"I'm sorry to |

"No." Jacob's eyes g[...]
to sound like I mind. I don't—not at all. I wish
I could do more. I just meant that I can't stop
thinking about you—" Jacob paused, color
rising in his cheeks. "That's not what I meant,
either."

A smile tickled Kate's lips. She hadn't seen
Jacob Dawson lose his composure once since
meeting him, and she rather enjoyed it now.
"It's okay."

Jacob shook his head and laughed
uncomfortably. "I should stop talking now."

"And I should get into the sanctuary."

She started down the hall again but stopped
when Jacob called out to her.

"I'm happy you decided to come, Kate."

For some reason, his words filled her with
incredible joy, and she turned to nod at him.
"So am I."

Kate turned back toward the hallway. A simple
attraction was nothing to worry about. She'd
denied the feelings for other men before, and
she could do it again.

There were more important things to worry
about.

Gabrielle Meyer lives in central Minnesota on the banks of the Mississippi River with her husband and four young children. As an employee of the Minnesota Historical Society, she fell in love with the rich history of her state and enjoys writing fictional stories inspired by real people and events. Gabrielle can be found at www.gabriellemeyer.com, where she writes about her passion for history, Minnesota and her faith.

Books by Gabrielle Meyer

Love Inspired

A Mother's Secret
Unexpected Christmas Joy

Love Inspired Historical

A Mother in the Making
A Family Arrangement
Inherited: Unexpected Family
The Gift of Twins

Visit the Author Profile page at Harlequin.com.

Unexpected Christmas Joy

Gabrielle Meyer

LOVE INSPIRED
INSPIRATIONAL ROMANCE

LOVE INSPIRED®
INSPIRATIONAL ROMANCE

ISBN-13: 978-1-335-55394-2

Unexpected Christmas Joy

Copyright © 2020 by Gabrielle Meyer

Recycling programs
for this product may
not exist in your area.

This is a work of fiction. Names, characters, places and incidents are either the
product of the author's imagination or are used fictitiously. Any resemblance
to actual persons, living or dead, businesses, companies, events or locales is
entirely coincidental.

This edition published by arrangement with Harlequin Books S.A.

For questions and comments about the quality of this book,
please contact us at CustomerService@Harlequin.com.

Love Inspired
22 Adelaide St. West, 40th Floor
Toronto, Ontario M5H 4E3, Canada
www.Harlequin.com

Printed in U.S.A.

Bear ye one another's burdens,
and so fulfil the law of Christ.
—*Galatians* 6:2

To my oldest daughter, Ellis. Your talent and joy on stage inspires me. Keep pursuing the dreams God has placed in your heart, Baby Belle!

Chapter One

Kate LeClair gripped her purse as sIhe looked through the shuttle bus windows to get a better glimpse of Bee Tree Hill. It wasn't the historic mansion or beautiful grounds that held her interest, but the people who were inside—or, more accurately, the eighteen-month-old triplets whom she'd never met but were now her sole responsibility.

The reality of where she was and what she was doing washed over her again and she had to take a deep breath to calm her nerves. Sunlight dappled the windows as the bus drove up the winding drive to the front door of the grand home. She was one of three strangers on the shuttle, and though the other two women had become friendly on the two-hour ride from the Minneapolis airport, Kate had kept to herself. She hadn't wanted to share details about the turn of events that led her to Timber Falls, Minnesota, because she hadn't had time to process them herself.

The driver stopped and the other two occupants openly admired the mansion as Kate gathered her purse and small carry-on bag.

"Is this your stop, dear?" asked the woman with a short silver bob.

"Yes."

"What a lovely home," said the other. "Is it yours?"

"No." Kate shook her head and smiled politely, unwilling to share any more details at the moment. She moved past them and stepped out of the van while the driver pulled her large suitcase from the back.

A brilliant blue sky peeked through the yellow-and-red leaves on the trees overhead. The air was cool and crisp and smelled like burning leaves. Friendly pumpkins and gourds sat near the steps in front of a bale of hay, offering a splash of color against the white-clapboard home.

"Have a good day," the driver said to Kate.

"Thank you." She handed him a tip and then faced the oversize front door of the mansion. "I'll try."

The people inside were grieving the loss of a

friend and about to hand over three little boys to a complete stranger. How could the day be good?

As the shuttle pulled away, Kate left her suitcase and carry-on at the bottom of the steps and climbed to the door. She pressed the buzzer and noticed her hands were trembling, so she clasped them together.

It didn't take long for the door to open. A pretty woman in her midtwenties appeared. Her blond hair was in a high pony and her brown eyes smiled in welcome. "Kate?" she asked.

Kate nodded. "Joy?"

"Yes. I'm Joy Asher." Joy opened the door wider. "Welcome to Bee Tree Hill. I hope you didn't have trouble finding us."

"Not at all." She motioned to her luggage. "Is it alright if I leave it here?"

"Of course." Joy moved aside for Kate to come into the house. "It will be fine there for a few minutes and I'm sure you're anxious to meet the boys."

Kate entered the front porch and barely had time to admire the leaded glass windows and painted beadboard before Joy motioned her to come into the foyer.

"You must be exhausted," Joy said to Kate. "So much has happened in the past twenty-four hours."

Kate tried to focus on the other woman, but

she was too busy searching for a glimpse of the toddlers.

"I told the social worker we'd be happy to keep the boys as long as necessary," Joy continued, "but she said you insisted on coming immediately."

Kate could only nod. In the past twenty-four hours, she had performed two live shows of *Les Misérables*, the national play she was currently traveling with, learned her only cousin was dead, inherited an old house with all of Tabby's belongings and become the legal guardian of three little boys. She'd also taken a six-week leave of absence, found a red-eye flight out of Charleston and been on two shuttle buses.

She hadn't slept for over thirty hours and she was beyond exhausted.

"...so I hope it's alright." Joy stopped talking and watched Kate with an expectant smile.

Kate shook her head, trying to focus. "I'm sorry, what were you saying?"

Joy nodded in understanding. "I said that Tabby's pastor—our pastor—has volunteered to be here in place of the social worker who was unexpectedly called away. Pastor Jacob lives across the street from Tabby's house—" She paused, grief lining her eyes. "Your house."

Her house. It didn't seem real. She didn't own

a house. She lived in an apartment in New York City—at least she did while she wasn't on tour.

"So I hope it's okay that he's here today," Joy said with a sweet smile. "I know how difficult this has been for you. We just want to be helpful."

"You've been more than helpful. Thank you." Kate didn't want to be rude, but she wanted to meet those boys. "Are the triplets here?"

"Yes," Joy said quickly. "I'm sorry. Of course you'd like to meet them. They're in the music room with Pastor Jacob." She motioned for Kate to follow her out of the foyer, through a sitting room and past a beautiful wall fountain.

The house was amazing and looked as if time had stood still. Every historical detail was in place, including the furnishings.

Joy took a left and Kate followed, facing a stunning room with high ceilings, tall windows and a shiny grand piano.

But none of those things held her interest long. Toddling around the room were three identical little boys—and one handsome pastor.

"Pastor Jacob," Joy said to the man who was sitting on the floor, playing with the boys. "Kate LeClair is here."

Pastor Jacob stood and Kate was amazed at how tall he was. His kind blue eyes made her feel just as welcome as Joy, and when he smiled, deep dimples lined his cheeks. "Hello, Kate. I'm Jacob Dawson."

She shook his outstretched hand, amazed at the size as it engulfed her own. "Hello."

But even the attractive pastor couldn't keep her attention from wandering to the boys.

Three identical pairs of blue eyes stared up at her. Kate could hardly remember what Tabby looked like, but she remembered her cousin's brilliant blue eyes, and saw them staring back at her now.

"And these are Tabby and Adam's boys," Joy said with a sad smile. She picked up the one closest to her. He giggled and pulled at the necklace around Joy's neck. "This is Aiken," she said. "He's the oldest, though by only eight minutes I've been told. He's the most curious and easiest to entertain."

"Aiken." Kate repeated his name, trying to appear calm when her heart was racing and her palms sweating. What if Joy handed the baby over to her? She hadn't held a child in years— not since she'd held her own baby girl moments after she was born. But Kate refused to let herself think of that heart-wrenching day when she'd given her only child up for adoption.

She had this day to think about instead.

"And this one is Bryce," Pastor Jacob said, lifting up the next baby. Bryce's eyes shined and he burrowed his face into the pastor's shirt. His thumb found his mouth and he sucked on it, peeking out at Kate in embarrassment. "He's a little bashful and quiet, but once he warms up, he's very affectionate."

"Bryce," Kate repeated, almost to herself. Aiken and Bryce.

"Carter is the one trying to escape." Joy laughed as she went after the little boy climbing the stairs to get out of the room. She reached down and scooped the second toddler up like it was no big deal and walked back to Kate with both boys in her arms.

"You look like you've done that before," Kate said in amazement.

"I have four-year-old twin daughters," Joy said with a shrug. "It's remarkable what you can do when you have no other choice."

For the first time, Kate noticed Joy's stomach under her loose blouse and realized she was expecting again. She didn't look like she was far along, but enough to notice. Kate couldn't stand around and let a pregnant woman hold two squirming babies.

It took all her willpower and a dose of prayer for Kate to step forward and offer to take one of the babies. "Would you like me to hold one?" she asked.

Joy handed over the runaway—Carter, if

Kate remembered correctly. The little boy didn't want to be in Kate's arms and made his opinion known quickly.

"Dow," he said, as he reached toward the floor and threw all his weight into his departure plan.

Kate's heart fell as she latched onto the slippery little guy a moment before he almost tumbled out of her arms.

"He's the one that will keep you on guard at all times," Pastor Jacob said, as he approached Joy and Kate. "He reminds me of my little girl, Maggie."

It took a few seconds for Kate's pulse to slow again. "I hate to admit this," she said to the other two, who looked completely at ease holding Aiken and Bryce, "but I have no idea what I'm doing." And it wouldn't pay to pretend—someone would be blind not to realize she was an inept caregiver. "I don't know what Tabby was thinking when she named me their guardian." If either of them actually knew Kate, they'd probably be laughing right about now. She had no business raising children. Hadn't her mom and ex-boyfriend made that clear when they told her to give up her daughter?

"Unfortunately, as you know, you're Tabby's only living relative and—" Joy looked to Pastor Jacob "—Adam's family has shown no interest in taking the babies, nor do I think Tabby and Adam would have wanted them to raise the boys." Joy bounced as she held Aiken on her hip. The movement was so natural that Kate doubted the other woman even noticed that she was doing it. "Besides, you'll catch on quickly. Just go easy on yourself." She smiled. "You'll see."

Kate didn't think she would—and didn't even know how long she'd be in Timber Falls to find out. Triplets were not part of her five-year plan. Her life wasn't conducive to raising children. Her apartment wasn't big enough—and she still had thirteen months on tour.

There were so many things to consider and it had all happened so quickly. All she could think at the time was she needed get to these motherless babies. She'd have to make the big decisions later—after she had more sleep.

"You've had a long twenty-four hours," Pastor Jacob said to Kate, as if reading her mind. "All of this has to be very overwhelming. If it's okay with you, I volunteered to take you and the boys back to Tabby's house."

"And I'll be over bright and early tomorrow morning to help you get settled," Joy promised. "I'd come tonight, but—"

"We're home!" At that moment, five noisy children ran into the room, all talking at once.

They were followed by an older woman who didn't seem to mind the chaos and smiled sweetly at Kate.

"Mrs. Thompson let us get ice-cream cones," one of the boys said.

"Kate, this is Mrs. Thompson, our dear family friend," Joy said to Kate. "More like a mother and grandmother, really."

"It's nice to meet you." Kate held tight to Carter, afraid the boy would try to plunge out of her grasp again, but she didn't want to be rude and not shake the lady's hand. She tried to maneuver her arm to hold the toddler and shake at the same time.

"No worries," Mrs. Thompson said with a laugh. "You've got your hands full."

The little girls, identical copies of each other, one in pink and one in purple, went to their mom. Aiken, Bryce and Carter all squealed with delight at seeing the kids. It was evident they were comfortable and familiar with them.

"We have parent–teacher conferences as soon as my husband comes home," Joy explained to Kate. "Or I'd be the one taking you home this afternoon. I'm sorry."

Kate's head began to pound and her eyes felt gritty. The lack of sleep was starting to catch up to her, and she sensed she had a long night ahead. "It's okay," she said. "We'll be fine. What time do you think you'll stop by tomorrow?"

"Tomorrow is Saturday, so the children will sleep in. I'll come after breakfast, so about eight?"

"In the morning?" Kate's eyes grew wide. After an evening performance, it wasn't unusual for her to get to sleep at one or two in the morning and then to rise about ten or eleven o'clock. Sleeping in for her was noon.

Joy just smiled. "The boys will probably wake you up a lot earlier than eight." She paused and then started again. "Oh, I forgot to mention that the social worker will also be coming tomorrow morning to meet with you and fill out some paperwork."

Kate could only nod. At this point, she probably wouldn't remember any of the details Joy had shared with her.

"If you're ready," Pastor Jacob said to Kate, "we could head over to the house now."

Kate continued to nod, though she hardly knew what she was doing anymore.

There were so many children that her head was spinning.

"I'll bring Aiken out to the minivan," Joy offered.

"Minivan?" Kate asked.

"Tabby and Adam had a minivan," Pastor Jacob explained. "I suppose it's yours now."

Kate would be expected to drive a minivan? She had her driver's license, only because she'd needed one when she was in high school, but she hadn't driven once since moving to New York.

"I'll drive the minivan over to the house," the pastor said as he led the way out of the mansion, all the children following them, talking and laughing. Pastor Jacob had to raise his voice to be heard over the noise. "I walked here earlier."

"Ryan," Joy called out, "can you grab the big suitcase, and, Jordan, can you get the smaller one?"

"What can I carry, Mama?" the youngest boy asked.

"You may carry the diaper bag, Kodi. It's that one by the door."

The little boy grabbed a backpack, a grin on his face.

A silver minivan sat beside the house and Pastor Jacob pulled a key fob from his pocket. He pressed a button and both of the side doors opened.

After all the babies were settled, and Carter made his opinion known about being tied into the car seat, Kate turned to Joy. "Thank you."

Joy leaned over and hugged Kate. "You have

my cell number. Do not hesitate to call, no matter the hour." She pulled back and leveled a no-nonsense mom-look at Kate. "I'm serious. You call me if you need me."

Kate couldn't help but smile, the first since she'd arrived. "I will."

"Good." She clasped her hands and put them up to her lips. "I'll be praying for you—and I'll bring some breakfast tomorrow morning when I come."

Pastor Jacob held the passenger door open and Kate got into the van.

"Everyone back inside!" Joy called to her brood, as she ushered them into the house and turned to wave one final time at Kate.

Pastor Jacob closed Kate's door and went around to the driver's side. He got into the minivan, and then paused as he looked at Kate. "Are you ready?"

"No."

He laughed, his kind eyes softening at the edges. "I don't blame you."

With the boys babbling in the back, and a stranger at the wheel, Kate gripped her purse on her lap once again. She wasn't ready—but life had taught her that it didn't matter.

Jacob turned out of Bee Tree Hill estate and onto Main Street, very aware of the young woman beside him. It took a lot for him to get nervous or feel self-conscious, but from the moment Kate LeClair had stepped into the music room at Bee Tree Hill, he'd felt like a bumbling idiot.

She couldn't be more than twenty-three or twenty-four, and despite the sleepless circles under her eyes, she was stunning. Her hair was thick and wavy and a dark shade of blond, but it was her eyes, which were large and expressive, that he had noticed first. He couldn't place the color, since they were almost the same shade as her hair.

The silence had gone on for too long as Jacob tried to pull himself together. He was a pastor—a professional—not a schoolboy who didn't know how to act in front of a pretty girl. He was helping her because it was his job and nothing more. "So, you're a Broadway performer." He'd been amazed when he'd learned about Kate's profession from Tabby a while ago. He never thought he'd actually meet her. "I've never known a professional actress."

Kate nodded as she took in the quaint downtown street. Row after row of brick buildings, large plate glass storefronts and flower baskets with mums filled Main Street.

"Is that something you've done for a while?" he asked, trying to keep her mind on something

that was safe and familiar—and not the three toddlers in the back seat. They'd consume her attention soon enough.

"I started acting in grade school," she said, finally looking at him. "I knew I wanted to be on Broadway when I was in high school, so I moved to New York after—" She paused and looked down at her purse. "It took me a long time to finally get a small role on Broadway. But it wasn't until last year that I started touring with *Les Misérables* as the character Fantine. We've been on tour for eleven months now."

"Wow. That's a long time to be away from home."

"The road becomes home, in a way," she said wistfully. "I travel with almost a hundred people, from actors to directors and stage crew. Many of them are as close as family."

Jacob shook his head at the thought. "It must be an amazing life."

She looked back at the downtown. "It can be."

What would she think of small, unassuming Timber Falls after she'd seen some of the biggest cities in America?

He came to a stop at the downtown intersection and flipped his blinker to turn right. "This is our Broadway," he said with a self-conscious smile. "Not quite the same as yours. This one runs across the Mississippi River and

connects the west side of town to the east side."
He turned east. "And there are no theaters on
this street—but it is home to Timber Falls Community Church, which is pretty special to me."

"Tabby's house is near a church, if I remember correctly," she said.

"Yes, right behind it, actually." Jacob tried
to sound nonchalant, though his pulse started
to speed up. "We had been trying to get Tabby
to sell the house to the church so we could expand."

Kate turned and studied Jacob. "But she
wouldn't?"

Jacob shook his head. "It's been in your family since it was built, apparently, and Tabby had
no plans on selling." Her refusal to sell hadn't
sat well with the church elders, though they had
offered more money than the house was worth.
The whole ordeal had almost caused Tabby
and Adam to leave Timber Falls Community
Church, but Jacob had been the one to finally
convince the elders to think of other options,
though they hadn't agreed on one yet. There
really weren't any to choose from.

"Why do they want to buy the house?" Kate
asked.

"To expand the church. There is a need for a
Christian school in Timber Falls and our church,
with its central location, is the ideal spot."

"So why not buy one of the other houses around the church?"

"There are no other houses," Jacob explained. "The church faces Broadway and sits on two city lots, wedged between Third and Fourth Street. Behind it are two more city lots. The historic Carnegie Library occupies one and your family home occupies the other."

"I think I remember now," Kate said. "I visited Timber Falls one summer when I was ten. I went to the library with Tabby almost every day." She rubbed her temples and squinted against the sun. "It was so long ago, some of my memory is fuzzy."

"I didn't know you were here before."

"It was only for a week." She glanced over her shoulder at the boys who had quieted for the car ride. They were now old enough for forward-facing car seats and Jacob could see each of them in the rearview mirror. "That was the only time I ever spent with Tabby," Kate continued. "We wrote letters back and forth through high school, but then—" She stopped again, just like she had before and seemed to reroute her conversation. "After high school we lost touch. Recently, I tried finding her on social media, but I don't think she was there."

"No." Jacob shook his head. "We had several

conversations about social media." He smiled. "Tabby was not a fan."

"I do remember she was a private person." Kate chuckled to herself. "Far different than my life." She paused for a moment. "I'm surprised the social worker was able to locate me. It's been years since Tabby and I spoke."

Jacob smiled. "Tabby knew exactly where you were all this time. She was very proud of who you became. She spoke of you often."

Kate bit her bottom lip, but did not respond.

"She had you listed as her next of kin in her will, so it wasn't hard for the social worker to find you."

He turned onto Third Street, a little pride swelling his chest. "There's the church," he said, pointing to the large Gothic-and-Tudor-style building. "It was built by the Asher family over a hundred years ago."

"Joy Asher's family?" she asked in amazement.

"Her husband's family, but yes, the same Ashers."

Jacob pulled the minivan to a stop next to the curb in front of the house. "And here's your family home. According to Tabby, it's been here just as long."

Kate looked out the window, shaking her head. "It's as lovely as I recall." She let out a sigh. "So picturesque. I remember how much I wanted to live in Timber Falls when I came to visit. I was so jealous that Tabby and her mom lived here when I was in a one-bedroom apartment in Chicago with my mom at the time."

"Were your mom and Tabby's mom sisters?"

"First cousins. If I remember correctly, it was their grandparents who built the house."

The Craftsman bungalow had been meticulously cared for by Tabby and Adam over the years. It was painted a dark gray and had a large dormer window facing the front. A covered porch, thick white trim around the doors and windows, and charming flower boxes filled with red mums were only some of the delightful characteristics of the big house. A white picket fence encircled the landscaped yard, and a two-story brick carriage house, used as the garage, sat near the alley, directly between the home and the library.

"And you live nearby?" she asked, turning to look at Jacob.

He pointed across the street at the blue Queen Anne Victorian-era home with its bay windows, tall gables and wraparound porch. "I live there with my seven-year-old daughter, Maggie. It's way too big for us, but it's the parsonage, so that's where we live." He loved the home, but it only reminded him that he and Maggie were alone in the world.

Instead of focusing on what he didn't have, though, he decided to change his course of thought. "Maggie's really excited to meet you. She wants to be an actress one day."

Kate offered a pretty smile. "I'd like to meet her, too."

Jacob was blindsided by the smile and struggled to find his voice.

One of the boys started to cry and wiggle to get out of his car seat.

"Should we get the boys inside?" he asked.

Taking a deep breath, Kate nodded. "It sounds like they're ready, even if I'm not."

Jacob pressed the buttons overhead to open the side doors and then he and Kate stepped out of the minivan.

"Just pinch those two buttons," Jacob said when he noticed she was struggling to get Carter out of his car seat. The little boy was straining against the harness holding him in place, causing Kate to clench her jaw.

"Here?" she asked.

Jacob nodded as he stepped into the mini-van, which wasn't an easy feat, given his height, and unbuckled Bryce from the back seat. He moved backward to exit the vehicle, knowing he probably looked like a giant getting out of a clown car, and then worked with one hand to free Aiken while still holding Bryce.

"How in the world did Tabby and Adam manage?" Kate asked, as she yanked on the harness to no avail.

"She didn't go out much," Jacob said matter-of-factly. "Though she was getting out more in the past couple of months since the boys were a little more manageable."

"This is manageable?" Kate shook her head, her eyes wide.

Carter was now throwing a fit, wanting out of his car seat.

Jacob rushed around the minivan and handed Aiken over to Kate. "Here, let me help."

Kate took the little boy, tears rimming her eyes. "I can't do this."

He pushed the button and the boy was free. Jacob scooped him up in his arms and Carter immediately settled.

"See?" Kate said. "I can't even get him out of his car seat. How am I supposed to take care of them when I can't do a simple thing like unhook a seat belt?"

"Remember, I've had years of experience." He tried to give her a reassuring smile. "You'll feel better when you get some rest. And I'm just across the street at any time."

She took another deep breath and nodded.

He admired her determination.

"I'll come out and get your luggage later." Jacob managed to press the sliding-door button on the key fob, thankful for the modern technology that made it possible to hold two squirming eighteen-month-old boys and close the minivan doors at the same time.

Kate unlatched the front gate and the five of them walked up the path to the enclosed porch.

"The key should be under the welcome mat," Jacob said to Kate.

"Seriously?"

He nodded.

"I thought people only did that on television." She shook her head. "Why lock the door if people know there's a key under the mat?"

"Since moving to Timber Falls, I've realized that locks are merely a formality." He grinned. "But the town is safe and most people don't have a need for them."

She leaned over, pulled aside the welcome mat and lifted up the key. "I'm starting to remember why I wanted to live here when I was a child."

"And now?" he asked. "Do you still feel that way?"

"I worked really hard for my life in New York." She let her gaze wander down Third Street where most of the homes were either

Craftsman or Victorian. The mature trees reached across the street and touched, their branches intertwined like clasped hands. Children played in a nearby park, parents pushed strollers toward the library and the church bell chimed five times, letting the kids know supper would be on the table soon.

Kate sighed. "I have so many decisions to make."

"Once you live here," Jacob said, "it's hard to leave." He knew that firsthand. He hated to think that he and Maggie would have to leave if he didn't fulfill his promise to start a school at Timber Falls Community Church within the year. It had been one of the stipulations the elders had given him when he'd been hired two years ago. They had given him a three-year plan, and in it they'd included the school. If it weren't built and ready to go by next September, he would be replaced. He needed to have a location ready by the first of the year, or they'd never have enough time.

That didn't give him long to convince Kate LeClair to sell—but now was not the time to ask.

Chapter Two

The smell was the first thing Kate remembered as she walked through the front door of Tabby's home. It was a mixture of pine-scented wood cleaner and the unmistakable smell of an old house. Sunshine spilled through the row of windows to her right, illuminating a spacious living room with thick walnut trim, built-in bookcases on either side of the generous brick fireplace and a large area rug. Directly ahead was the long hallway to the back of the house and a wide straight stairway. To her left was the dining room with the bay window and the same rich walnut trim. On either side of the hall, half walls and beautiful wood pillars gave it the mark of the Craftsman-style Kate had loved since first seeing the home.

"Nothing has changed," she said to Pastor Jacob as he followed her into the house.

Nothing and everything.

"Welcome home," he said with a smile.

The little boy she held squirmed in Kate's arms and jumped with excitement at being home. She wasn't sure which one he was, since all three boys were dressed in identical outfits, but she knew it wasn't Carter. Carter was the one in Pastor Jacob's arms pushing and wiggling to get loose. He had been the one fussing in the car seat when she couldn't get him out.

All three boys squealed and bounced at being home. "Mamamama," one of them said, looking all around the house for his mother.

Tears sprang to Kate's eyes and she swallowed the lump in her throat. There was no way the boys could understand their parents weren't coming home again. A fierce sense of protection overwhelmed her and she wanted to pull all three boys close to comfort them.

"Why don't we set the boys down in the toy room?" Pastor Jacob asked Kate, as he entered the living room and walked toward the back of the house. "They might enjoy seeing some of their familiar toys." He nodded toward the back room, which was separated from the living room by the same half walls and pillars. "The room back here used to be a den, but Tabby turned it into a toy room. There are gates at the entrances to keep them from crawling through the house."

Kate followed him, noticing the pictures on the walls, the built-in shelves and the tabletops. She paused when she saw a picture of Tabby's little family. Kate had never met Adam and was seeing him for the first time. He was a nice-looking man with a kind face—but it was her cousin Tabby who drew Kate's full attention. She was just as beautiful as Kate remembered, though fourteen years older.

A whole flood of memories resurfaced in Kate's mind and heart. "Oh, Tabs," she said under her breath. Why had Kate let the years and her mistakes separate them?

Pastor Jacob stepped over the gate and set the boys down on the colorful mat covering the wood floor. The boys instantly went to their toys and began to play.

"Here," he said to Kate. "I'll take Aiken."

Kate handed over the little boy, trying to take a mental note of the boys to remember who was who. "How do you know he's Aiken?" she asked.

"It's easy, once you get to know them." Pastor Jacob set the little boy down. "Aiken has a little scar by his eye from when he fell a few months ago trying to walk."

Aiken, scar.

"And Bryce has a small mole on his earlobe," Pastor Jacob continued. "Plus, he usually has his thumb in his mouth."

Bryce, mole. Thumb.

"And Carter." He laughed and shook his head as the little boy picked up a small basketball and whipped it toward the hoop. "He doesn't have either of those things—but he has a lot of energy."

Carter, energy.

Kate would never remember.

"I think it's safe to leave them in here for a few minutes as I show you around." Pastor Jacob motioned for her to follow him through the other opening and into the back hall.

"Thank you for all your help, Pastor Jacob," Kate said. "But I can't ask you to give up your entire evening."

"Just call me Jacob," he said. "And it's no trouble."

Just Jacob. She liked that. There was something very warm and comfortable about Jacob Dawson, as if she'd known him for years. He must be a well-liked pastor.

"But if you'd rather be alone with the boys right now, I understand." He watched her closely, waiting for her to decide.

She didn't want to be alone with the boys, but it would have to happen sooner than later.

His phone dinged. "Sorry about that." He pulled it out of his back pocket. "I'll just turn off the ring—" He frowned as he scanned the message.

"Is everything okay?"

"It's a text about Maggie's babysitter—from her husband." He continued to frown. "It looks like Mrs. Meacham has fallen and broken her hip." He put his phone back. "I'm sorry, but I need to go to the hospital."

"I completely understand."

Kate followed him through the hall and toward the front door, passing the stairs as they went.

"Oh, here." He stopped and turned.

She came to an abrupt halt as he handed her the keys to the minivan.

"You might want to take it off the street and park in the garage," he advised. "The street sweeper comes through early in the morning."

She took the keys, trying not to feel panicked at the idea of being alone with the boys—or driving a minivan.

One of them started to fuss in the other room.

"Here's my card," he said, as he pulled his wallet from his pocket and took out a card. "The second number is for my cell phone. Call or text if you need anything."

Kate nodded and began to follow him again.

"Goodbye, Kate." He opened the door and then paused again. "I'll be praying for you and the boys."

With that, Jacob left.

She closed the door and stood in the foyer for a moment, the weight of the situation lying heavy on her shoulders.

Another boy started to cry in the toy room and her heart began to beat faster. Were they hungry? Did they need their diapers changed? Were they sad? What did they need and how would she know?

Taking a deep breath, she turned and walked back down the hall toward the crying toddlers.

Now that she was in Timber Falls, she had so many things to decide and accomplish.

But right now, she just needed to get the boys to stop crying.

Two of the three were standing at the gate in the hallway. One was sucking his thumb and the other was shaking the gate, trying to loosen it as he cried. The third toddler was sitting in the middle of the toy room pulling diaper wipes out of a container. They were in a mound on the floor next to him.

Where did he get the wipes?

He took one and shoved it toward his mouth.

"No, no." Kate leaped over the gate—and the

other two boys—and pulled the wipe from him a moment after it touched his lips.

His little mouth flew open and he immediately began to cry. Large tears fell from his eyes as he sat there and wailed.

The other two continued their own pitiful cries and tears filled Kate's eyes, as well. She quickly gathered the wipes and prayed they weren't harmful. Setting them on one of the shelves, she turned to face the three little boys.

"What do you want?" she asked.

The one who had tried to eat the wipes—Aiken, if she remembered correctly—lifted his hands toward her.

Her heart melted as she picked him up and held him close. She was a complete stranger, but she was the only one there to offer love and affection.

His tears started to subside, but hers did not.

Maybe they were hungry. She was starving. She hadn't eaten since early that morning at the airport in South Carolina.

"Let's find something to eat," she said to them.

Of course, they didn't respond, though she hadn't expected them to.

But what did they eat? Did they have bottles? Did they eat solid food? She had no experience with children.

And what did she do with them until the meal was ready?

She stepped over the crying babies and into the hall, still holding Aiken. The other two continued to cry as she entered the kitchen.

Three high chairs lined one wall.

Setting Aiken in one, she secured him with the buckles and then went back to get the other two. She had no idea how to carry or lift two of them at the same time, so she took one into the kitchen, secured him in the chair and then went back for the third.

After she had them all in their high chairs, and her ears were ringing from their crying, she pulled open the cupboards. The first one contained baby food in individual containers. Some of them were chunky food, like carrots and peaches.

At least she knew they could eat solid food.

She took some containers out of the cupboard, opened them and then drained the juice into the sink. Not knowing if she should heat the carrots, and not wanting to take the time, she found three colorful plastic plates in the dishwasher and put some of each food on the plates. It wasn't fancy, but it would have to do. She placed the plates in front of the boys and turned to find forks, but the boys immediately quieted and started to grab the food with their fists.

Kate sank into a kitchen chair, her head pounding, thankful for a bit of silence.

And then she smelled an unmistakable scent—one that made her eyes water.

She'd have to find the diapers—and the sooner the better.

"But I want to meet her, Daddy," Maggie said to Jacob as he pulled up to their house an hour after he'd received the text message from Mr. Meacham. "Is she pretty?"

"I've already told you we need to give Miss LeClair some privacy. She's had a big day." He ignored the second question.

"But she's probably hungry and we have this whole pizza all to ourselves." Maggie blinked her big blue eyes at Jacob in the rearview mirror. "We should share, shouldn't we?"

Truth be told, Jacob had felt bad about leaving Kate all alone, and so abruptly. He didn't know if she had experience with children, but one way or the other, three at one time could be very overwhelming.

Maybe he and Maggie could make a neighborly call—and offer her some pizza.

"Alright," he said to his daughter. "Let's take the pizza over and see if she needs some help."

"Yay!" Maggie unlatched her seat belt and started to climb out of her booster seat.

"But—" he looked over his shoulder at his seven-year-old daughter "—if she doesn't want us there, we're leaving. No protesting, do you hear?"

Maggie grinned and opened her door. "Yes, sir," she said, as she jumped out of the car.

"Wait for me," Jacob called to her as she raced through their yard toward Kate's house.

Jacob took the pizza box off the passenger seat and closed the doors, then he followed Maggie, who waited impatiently on the sidewalk in front of their house.

Nerves started to get the better of him as they crossed the street. Even though he'd spent the past hour with Mr. and Mrs. Meacham, praying for healing and peace as Mrs. Meacham prepared for surgery on her hip, Jacob's mind hadn't strayed far from Kate LeClair. It had been a long time since an attractive woman had caught his attention. It hadn't happened since he'd met his wife, Laura, his freshman year of college. She had been gone for five and a half years now, and Jacob had started to wonder if anyone would ever turn his head again.

He'd never expected it to be a Broadway star living across the street from the parsonage.

As they walked up the sidewalk to Kate's

house, he chided himself for his foolish thoughts. It didn't really matter how attractive Miss LeClair was—Jacob had made a promise to himself when Laura died that he'd dedicate his life to his daughter and to the church. The kind of love story he and Laura had only came once in a lifetime. He'd be selfish to ask for it again—and, the truth was, he didn't deserve to fall in love. If he hadn't been such a selfish husband, Laura wouldn't be dead, and he wouldn't be raising Maggie without her mama. He could never take that chance again.

Maggie rang the doorbell and jumped from one foot to the other in excitement. Her blond ponytail bounced and her blue eyes glowed. "I'm going to meet a real actress, Daddy."

"I know, sweetheart."

"I want to be an actress one day," she said, as if announcing it for the first time.

He put his hand on her head. "I know."

They stood there for a long time, the pizza hot in Jacob's hand. A mom and dad walked past, the mom pushing a stroller while the dad kept his eye on a little boy with training wheels on his bike. Cars drove past the church on Broadway and a bird swooped overhead and landed on a tree on the boulevard.

"Maybe she's gone to bed," Jacob said.

"Let's try the kitchen door." Maggie didn't

wait for him to protest and jumped off the front stoop.

"Maggie," Jacob called after her, but Maggie disappeared around the house.

Jacob followed, stepping over a water hose. The grass would need to be mowed soon and the leaves picked up. He'd try to find the time tomorrow.

He turned the corner right as Maggie knocked on the kitchen door.

"You need to listen to me when I call your name," he told his daughter.

"I hear the boys crying." Maggie put her ear to the door.

"I hear it, too."

"See." Maggie crossed her arms. "She does need our help."

Kate appeared at the door and looked through the glass at them. Exhaustion lined her face as she opened the door.

The sound of the boys' cries escalated.

"I don't know what they want," she said in tears. "I fed them and changed Carter's diaper, but they won't stop crying."

"They want their sippy cups." Maggie pushed past Kate and entered the kitchen. "They're in this cupboard."

Upon seeing Maggie, Aiken and Bryce stopped

crying, but Carter didn't open his eyes long enough to see their new visitor.

Maggie pulled a step stool up to the cabinet and opened the door. She took out three plastic sippy cups and lids, then she climbed down the stool and went to the refrigerator.

"She came over and helped Tabby as often as I'd let her," Jacob explained to Kate when she turned a questioning gaze to him. "She loves the boys." He tried to offer her a reassuring smile and then remembered why they'd come. "Are you hungry? Would you like some pizza?"

"I'm starving." She opened the door wider. "Thank you."

Jacob entered the kitchen and set the box down on the counter.

Maggie pulled a gallon of whole milk out of the refrigerator. It was full and she struggled to get it up on the counter, so Jacob took over. He checked the expiration date and saw it was still good, so he poured milk into each cup and put the lids on, then he handed them to the boys who were still in their high chairs. They immediately stopped crying and began to drink.

"That's all they wanted?" Kate asked.

"Food, milk, diaper change, naps." Jacob opened the pizza box. "You'll figure it all out."

Maggie stood in front of the boys, talking to each one in a soft, soothing tone.

"She's a natural," Kate said in awe.

"Mags," Jacob called to his daughter, "I'd like you to meet Miss LeClair."

Maggie grew bashful then, which was so unlike her. Jacob smiled. Her cheeks turned pink and she ducked her head. "Hello, Miss LeClair."

"This is Maggie," Jacob said to Kate. "She wants to be an actress."

Despite her exhaustion, Kate offered Maggie a big smile. It was just like the one she'd given Jacob earlier in the car and it had the exact same effect on him.

"It's nice to meet you, Maggie. If it's alright with your dad, you may call me Kate."

Maggie looked up at Jacob for approval. He nodded.

"May I come and help with the boys?" Maggie asked Kate.

"I'd love your help." Kate looked to Jacob. "That is, if your dad doesn't mind."

"I know!" Maggie jumped up and down, her earlier embarrassment forgotten. "May I come here after school, Daddy? Mrs. Meacham said she won't be well for a long time."

Kate watched Jacob, something akin to desperation in her face.

"Maggie usually goes to Mrs. Meacham's after school for a couple hours Monday through Friday, until I'm done with work."

"She could come here," Kate said quickly. "I'd appreciate the help."

"Are you sure?" Jacob didn't want Maggie to be more of a burden than necessary.

"I'm positive."

"Please, Daddy." Maggie wrapped her hands together and begged him.

"If it's alright with Miss—with Kate, then it's alright with me." He met Kate's gaze. "And I'll just be at the church, so if something comes up, she can always come over to the church with me."

Kate nodded, and it seemed as if a weight had lifted from her shoulders.

"It'll just be until Mrs. Meacham is able to care for her again," Jacob said. "The doctor said six or eight weeks at the most."

"I only have a six-week leave of absence," Kate told Jacob. "I'm rejoining the cast when they come to Minneapolis at the end of December."

Jacob frowned. "I just assumed you'd be staying."

She looked away from Jacob and toward the boys. "Everything's happened so quickly. I haven't made any definite plans, but I—I don't plan to stay in Timber Falls."

"But the boys?" He shook his head, confused. What would she do with the boys?

"I don't know yet." She spoke so softly he almost didn't hear her.

It wasn't the time to press her to make decisions—nor did he have the right. He felt protective of the boys, because Tabby and Adam had been members of his church, but the truth was he didn't have any rights to the triplets or any say over what happened to them.

"I appreciate the pizza," Kate said, changing the subject.

"Help yourself." Jacob turned the box toward her. "When we're done eating, Maggie and I can help you get the boys ready for bed."

Carter's eyelids were already starting to droop and Aiken had drained his milk. He tossed the empty cup on the floor and said, "All done."

Maggie giggled and picked up the cup with a piece of pizza in her other hand.

Kate also smiled, though hers seemed more of a polite gesture. When she looked at the triplets, a combination of panic and awe radiated from her face.

It was evident that Kate had little to no experience with children—and she'd need Jacob and Maggie's help.

Jacob didn't mind at all.

Chapter Three

Jacob didn't usually work on Saturdays, but today the church ladies were coming for their fall cleaning. He had learned the hard way that if he wasn't there to supervise, they would feel free to rearrange his office and throw out things they felt were useless.

"Do I have to go to the church with you?" Maggie asked, as she skipped across the street toward the church with Jacob. The air was cool and she was wearing a thick brown sweater. "Can I go to Kate's and help with the babies?"

"She's not expecting you." He took her hand. "And, besides, the church ladies like having you around."

Maggie wrinkled her nose. "They pinch my cheeks and call me *honey*."

"That's how they show they love you."

"Can we please stop to see if Kate needs my

help?" she asked, tugging on his hand to pull him toward the gray bungalow.

Joy Asher's conversion van was parked near the curb in front of the house. No doubt she was there helping Kate. "Mrs. Asher is there," Jacob said. "You can come to the church. Maybe we'll stop by later and check in on her."

The look of disappointment on Maggie's face squeezed at Jacob's heart, but he knew he couldn't always give in to his daughter. It was a constant tug he experienced—trying to discipline her, while keeping her happy. The guilt he felt over raising her as a single dad shouldn't make him soft, but he knew he gave in to his daughter far too often.

They continued inside through the back door of the church, which was already unlocked. No doubt Mrs. Caruthers had arrived at the break of day to get a head start on the others. It was a continuous competition between the older ladies as to who could serve better and faster.

"Yoo-hoo. Is that you Pastor Jacob?" Mrs. Caruthers called out to him from somewhere within the church almost before he and Maggie entered the building.

Maggie looked up at Jacob, her eyes large. "How does she know it's us?" she whispered.

Jacob put his finger up to his lips to silence the child and only smiled.

Mrs. Caruthers appeared with a red handkerchief over her gray hair and an apron tied around her thick waist. "I've already started polishing the pews in the sanctuary. I thought I'd be done by now, but Mr. Johnson showed up twenty minutes ago to speak to you and I couldn't let him wait alone." She crossed her arms and nodded. "So we enjoyed a cup of coffee and some donuts I made fresh last night."

"Mr. Johnson is here?" Jacob had no wish to talk to the head elder. He knew why he'd come and he didn't have any answers for him.

"He's waiting in your office." She turned her focus on Maggie. "Well, hello, honey." She came forward and Maggie stepped closer to Jacob's leg. "I put extra chocolate frosting on your donut." She pinched Maggie's cheek and clucked her tongue. "You're getting so grown up."

Maggie looked up at Jacob, exasperation on her little face.

The back door opened and three more women entered, all talking as fast as they could.

"Mary Lou Caruthers." Mrs. Topper shook her head and wiggled her pointer finger. "We told you eight thirty and not one minute sooner."

Mrs. Caruthers ran her hand over the front of her apron and tried not to smile. "You know me. Once I'm awake, I can't be idle for a moment."

Mrs. Topper's lips pursed and she set her coat on the hooks near the door. "I should have known you'd come earl—oh, Maggie!" She turned to the little girl at the same moment the others noticed Jacob's daughter. They swarmed around her and she endured their attention with a forlorn look, making Jacob wish he had let her go to Kate's, after all.

"You go on, Pastor," Mrs. Evans told Jacob. "We'll take care of Maggie while you get your work done."

"Before you go." Mrs. Anderson put her hand on Jacob's sleeve. "Is it true that Tabby's cousin arrived yesterday?"

Suddenly, that's all the other women were interested in, as well.

"Yes."

"And did you meet her?" Mrs. Caruthers asked.

"I showed her to her home."

Their eyes grew wide at the news.

"And is she single?" Mrs. Topper asked, raising an eyebrow.

Jacob knew where their minds were going and he needed to stop them before they got there.

"She's very overwhelmed right now." He started to move toward his office, which was down the hall, facing the back of the church. His window looked directly toward Kate's house with a view of his own.

"But she's single?" Mrs. Anderson asked. "And is she pretty?"

"She's an actress, I hear," Mrs. Evans said. "So, of course, she'll be pretty."

The others nodded in agreement.

"So she's single?" Mrs. Caruthers asked.

Jacob wouldn't get away without answering them, so he simply shrugged. "I don't think she's married."

They tittered at the news and began to speak among themselves. The church ladies were notorious for playing matchmaker—whether two people wanted to be matched or not. They were relentless and single-minded. After two years, they had finally stopped pestering him about Evelyn Ramsey, one of the single women who attended church regularly.

Jacob looked to Maggie, questioning her with his eyes. Did she want to stay with the church ladies or come with him? She just shrugged in surrender.

He winked at her and then walked down the hall toward his office. His door had a window and he saw Rick Johnson standing near the exterior window, looking at Kate's house. He wore a pair of khaki pants and a polo shirt and had his hands in his pockets.

Jacob pushed open the door, mindful that he'd locked it the night before and either Rick or Mrs. Caruthers had taken the liberty to unlock it.

Rick turned. "Pastor," he said. "I've been waiting for you."

"Hello, Rick." Jacob closed his office door and motioned for the elder to take a seat in one of the wooden chairs across from Jacob's desk.

Rick sat and crossed his ankle over his knee. He combed his thinning hair over his balding scalp and wore a large class ring on his right pinkie.

Jacob took his seat and gave Rick his full attention. "What brings you in today?"

"I think you know why I'm here." He didn't smile. "Have you had a chance to talk to Miss LeClair about selling the house?"

Leaning back in his chair, Jacob sighed. "I have spoken to her, but I have not asked her to sell."

"Why not?"

"Her world was turned upside down in the past couple of days. She'll need some time to settle in before she is able to make decisions." He clasped his hands together. "I think it's best to wait."

"And I think we've waited long enough." Rick gripped his ankle and the ruby in his ring shined in the light. "My oldest son will be a senior in high school next year," Rick said. "I'd like him to be in the first graduating class at Timber Falls Christian School. My wife and I have served here diligently for the past fifteen years and we've given this church thousands of dollars. I don't think it's an unreasonable request." He paused and his face grew even more serious. "And, more than that, you made a promise to the elders that you'd have the school built before next year."

"I've tried—"

"Stop trying and start doing." Rick stood. "I've made myself clear and you know what the elders expect." He went to the door and opened it. "See that it's taken care of."

Without saying goodbye, Rick left Jacob's office.

A movement caught Jacob's eyes and he looked toward Kate's house. She stood near the window in the toy room, her back facing the church.

Jacob hated to approach her so soon about selling, but he also hated to disappoint the elder board. Maybe he'd pay her a visit after Joy left and invite Kate to church in the morning. It might not hurt to bring up the sale of the house. Maybe it would help her decide what to do once her leave of absence was over.

Kate stood at the front door and waved at Joy as she pulled away from the house in her large van.

Joy had walked her through the entire house, shown her where everything was from the Q-tips to the toilet paper and even written a detailed schedule for Kate to follow with the babies. She had also brought groceries to fill the fridge and cupboards so Kate wouldn't have to worry about shopping anytime soon.

Along with Joy, the social worker had come to the house and met Kate. There had been some forms to fill out and the lady had told Kate what to expect from a legal point of view. If Kate was agreeable, she would have full legal and physical custody of the boys. Kate had been honest with the social worker, and with Joy, and had shared her concerns about raising the boys. They all agreed to meet again in four weeks for Kate to give her final decision.

Before leaving, Joy had helped Kate get the boys to take a nap and now Kate was ready to pass out.

Closing the door, she stood in the hall for a moment and just looked at the house. It was such a bittersweet experience to return to this home that her great-grandparents had built. She hadn't thought she'd ever be here again—but the reason she'd come laid heavy upon her heart. As soon as she had a chance, she wanted to find the cemetery where Tabby and Adam were buried that past week and pay her respects. She had learned from Joy that the couple had finally taken a night away from the boys, leaving them with a babysitter for the first time, and traveled to a nearby town for a date. On the way home, they'd been hit by a driver who had fallen asleep at the wheel.

Kate walked into the living room and sank onto the couch.

A video monitor sat on the coffee table and she could see the boys in their cribs and hear the subtle sounds of them sleeping.

All around her, the house was exactly as Tabby and Adam had left it. Decades of history filled the rooms. Original furniture was mingled with a flat-screen television, vintage rugs were interspersed with a modern stereo and the walls were full of pictures of every generation of the family. Kate had even found a framed picture of her and Tabby from the summer she'd visited hanging on the stair wall.

If she did sell the house, she'd have to go through everything and decide what to do with it all. She'd have to decide what to keep for the boys, what to sell and what to give away.

The task felt daunting—and sleep sounded so nice right about now. She lay down and nuzzled the throw pillow right when the doorbell rang.

Jumping up, she ran to the door so whoever

was there wouldn't ring it again and wake up the babies.

Looking through the glass window on the door, she saw Jacob Dawson standing on the stoop outside the covered porch.

He grinned and her frustration at being interrupted from a nap melted away.

Kate opened the door and motioned him to come into the porch. A white swing hung from chains in the corner and large braided rugs were on the wood floor. Sunlight poured through the windows and rested on Jacob's face as he stepped inside.

"I hope I'm not bothering you," he said, as he walked over the threshold with Maggie at his side.

"Not at all." She couldn't tell him the truth. Besides, she liked seeing him again.

"I just thought I'd check to see if you needed anything." He motioned behind him. "We were heading home for lunch."

"Joy was just here," she said. "She brought food and showed me what I might need for the boys." She smiled. "I think I'm set for a bit."

He nodded and shuffled his feet as he looked down at Maggie and then back to Kate.

"Did *you* need something?" she asked, sensing that he'd come for a different purpose.

"I—uh—wanted to extend an invitation to

church." He indicated the church to his right. "We'd love to see you there. Sunday school starts at nine and the service begins at ten thirty." He swallowed and continued. "Everyone would love to meet you, and the boys know many people there already. We have a nursery, so you could drop them off and get a couple hours to yourself."

Kate glanced at the building, which loomed large and impressive next door. It was at the Timber Falls Community Church where Kate had given her heart to Jesus as a little girl. She'd been gifted with a Bible and taught how to read it, but after they left Timber Falls, Kate had rarely been in church. It was never a priority for her mother, and after becoming pregnant as a teenager, she felt too soiled. Would she fit in? Would people know she didn't belong?

"There's no pressure," Jacob said quickly. "I just thought I'd let you know you're more than welcome."

"And I really, really want you to come!" Maggie said with a grin.

Kate couldn't stop herself from smiling back at the enthusiastic child. "I attended church there with Tabby when we were kids," she said, not wanting to disappoint her new neighbor— or his bright-eyed daughter who watched her expectantly.

"So you'll come?" he asked.

Kate looked over her shoulder toward the inside of the house where the boys were still sleeping. "I don't know if I can get the boys out the door that early, but I'll try."

"Yay!" Maggie said, jumping up and down.

Jacob looked truly pleased and for some reason, it made warmth fill Kate's chest.

"There's something else." Jacob's smile faded. "I really didn't want to ask so soon, but I thought it might help you in making your decisions."

She watched him closely, a slight frown drawing her brows together. "What do you want to ask?"

"I mentioned the church tried buying this house from Tabby and Adam."

"You said Tabby didn't want to sell."

"Right." He took a deep breath. "And I don't want to put any pressure on you, but the elders are still interested in purchasing the home—if you're willing to sell."

Kate nibbled on her bottom lip. Was this the answer she needed? She didn't have a reason for keeping the house—but what would Tabby think? What if her cousin had wanted to keep the house to pass on to her boys? They were the fifth generation in the family to live there. Was it selfish of Kate to want to sell?

She opened her mouth to tell Jacob she'd consider selling, but the words wouldn't come. She'd spent the past fourteen years wishing she had grown up in Timber Falls, in this very house, and now that she was here, why would she want to sell? What if this was God's way of answering her little-girl prayers? Once she sold the house, there would be no going back—especially if the church tore it down.

"I don't know what I'm going to do, yet," Kate answered honestly. "If I decide to sell, you'll be the first to know."

He nodded. "That's what I thought. But I wanted to make sure."

"Can I play with the boys?" Maggie asked Kate.

"They're sleeping," she said.

"We should get going." Jacob put his hand on Maggie's shoulder. "So you can rest a little, too."

Kate didn't want to look so relieved, but she couldn't stop herself from sighing and leaning against the door frame. A nap sounded so nice.

"Bye!" Maggie waved as she and Jacob stepped outside.

"Hopefully we'll see you tomorrow at church," Jacob added.

"I'll try."

"Don't try," Maggie said with a decisive nod. "Just do it."

Jacob looked sharply at his daughter, a frown on his face. "Where'd you hear that?"

"Mr. Johnson—when he was talking to you in his office."

"It's not polite to eavesdrop or to speak that way to Kate."

Maggie dipped her head. "I'm sorry, Kate."

"It's okay." Kate smiled at Jacob, hiding the giggle that wanted to escape.

He returned the smile, shaking his head, and then left.

She stepped back into the house and walked toward the couch, where the sound of the babbling boys echoed from the monitor.

They were awake.

Kate leaned against the pillar and put her face in her hands.

She would not give in to tears.

Pushing away from the pillar, she straightened her shoulders and said a prayer. If God had brought her to Timber Falls, and into this home to care for those boys, then He would give her the strength to do the job.

At least, she hoped He would.

There was no way of knowing unless she tried.

Or, as Maggie said, unless she just did it.

Chapter Four

On Sunday morning, the sun shone bright in the brilliant blue sky as Kate fastened Carter into the front of the long stroller and then straightened to face the back of the church. Already, Aiken and Bryce were secure in their seats behind Carter, and Kate had no more excuses to miss the morning service. She had tried to think of a dozen different reasons why she shouldn't go, but the truth was she wanted to be there. She wanted to recapture part of the memories she had made the first time she was in Timber Falls—and she wanted to see if there was a way to grow closer to God, something she had desired all of her life.

It didn't hurt that the pastor was nice to look at and she couldn't stop wondering what it would be like to hear him preach.

The babies babbled as Kate pushed the stroller

toward the building next door. She had watched the cars pull into the parking lot and line the street in front of her home earlier that day in preparation for Sunday school, but she wasn't quite ready to tackle such an intimate classroom setting with a bunch of strangers. Instead, she had waited until 10:15 a.m. to head over for the service. Maybe that way she could just sneak in the back, listen to Jacob's sermon and then sneak out without being noticed.

Kate pushed the stroller through the gate and into the alley separating her lawn from the church parking lot. She wasn't the only person coming late for the service, so she smiled at a young family as they walked toward the back door.

"Hello," the mom called out to Kate. She wore a dark blue jean jacket over a pretty floral dress. "You must be Kate," she said.

Kate had no idea who the woman was, so she simply nodded as she walked through the parking lot toward the church door.

"We've heard so much about you," the lady continued. "Welcome to Timber Falls."

"Thank you."

"Here." The woman's husband opened the back door all the way. "Let me help you get the stroller inside."

"Thank you." Kate wondered how she would

have managed without their help. The stroller wasn't bulky, or unmanageable, but it did take a little maneuvering to get it through the door.

"I'm Amber," the lady said, extending her hand to Kate. "And this is my husband, Eric."

"It's nice to meet you." They stood in a back hall with coat hooks lining the wall. Amber's three children took off their jackets and set them on the lower hooks, as if they'd done it a hundred times before.

"I'm heading to the nursery, if you'd like to come with me." Amber's smile was wide and contagious. "We're so excited you're here. Samantha told me you're a Broadway actress."

Samantha? Who was Samantha?

"Yes, I am."

"That's amazing! Tabby mentioned her cousin was an actress, but I didn't know you were famous."

Kate's cheeks grew warm. "I wouldn't call myself famous."

"When Roxanne told Samantha, she couldn't believe it, either," Amber continued, appearing not to hear Kate as she walked her down a long hallway, past several classrooms with colorful biblical posters indicating what ages and grades met in the rooms. "Apparently, Tabby did tell Piper, but Piper never bothered to tell any of us, which isn't that strange, since she's so busy remodeling that big old bed-and-breakfast and doesn't get to church as often as the rest of us." She laughed and Kate smiled uncomfortably, knowing she'd never remember all these names.

"Here we are." Amber pointed to a door leading into a bright and sunny room full of toddlers. "You can check the boys in here. My children are in a different room. We'll see you soon! I can't wait to hear all about Broadway. Nice to meet you, Kate." Amber turned and gathered her children to her side as she ushered them down the hall to another room.

Before Kate could catch her breath, an older woman grinned at her from behind a tall counter. "Well, hello! I was hoping to see the triplets today."

Aiken, Bryce and Carter all clapped and wiggled to get out of their harnesses and into the arms of the cheerful women who greeted them in the nursery.

Kate started to unbuckle Carter. "I'm afraid I don't know the protocol for leaving the boys—"

"Oh, go on into the sanctuary, dear," said one of the ladies, coming around the counter and shooing Kate away. "We'll get them all checked in and have them ready to go for you when the service is over."

"Thank you." Kate let out a weary sigh. It would be nice to have a few minutes to herself.

"Just head on back down the hallway," the lady said, "until you come to the front lobby. Grab yourself a cup of hot coffee and a donut. Everyone gathers there before the service starts."

Nodding her thanks, Kate left the boys and walked down the hall. She passed several more families on their way to drop off their children. Many of them said hello or simply smiled.

She wasn't in any hurry to get to the gathering space and face another round of strangers who knew her. She had a feeling Amber's friends wouldn't be too far away.

A room caught her attention, because it wasn't like the others. It was an office with a name painted on the pane of glass. Pastor Jacob Dawson it said in bold print.

Kate glanced through the window and found a very neat desk, a couple of plants and a comfortable-looking couch. Behind the desk, a built-in shelf displayed dozens of books, a few plaques and several pictures. She smiled when she saw one of Maggie, grinning, with a missing bottom tooth. But her smile faded when she noticed a picture of a beautiful woman holding a small infant in a pink blanket. For the first time, Kate wondered about Maggie's mom—Jacob's wife. Was that her in the picture?

"Her name was Laura," a deep voice said just

behind her. "She died when Maggie was eighteen months old."

Kate's pulse picked up its pace as she turned and looked into Jacob's handsome face. His smile was both sad and deeply kind—a combination that endeared him to her and made her wonder what he had tucked away in that big heart of his.

"She was beautiful."

Jacob laughed. "She was also incredibly brilliant and didn't feel bad about beating me at trivia games."

"Maggie looks like her."

"A blessing I am eternally grateful for." His smile deepened, widening his dimples. "No little girl should walk through life looking like me."

Her impulse was to tell him he was a handsome man, but she kept her words to herself, very aware that he was the pastor of this bustling church.

She stepped away from the door. "You're probably busy—I should get out of your way."

"I just forgot my sermon notes on my printer." He pulled a key out of his pocket and unlocked the office door, a sheepish twinkle in his eyes. "I'm usually not this forgetful, but I've been a little preoccupied thinking about my neighbor lately."

Heat warmed Kate's cheeks. "I'm sorry to be so much trouble."

"No." Jacob's eyes grew wide. "I didn't mean to sound like I mind—I don't—not at all. I wish I could do more. I just meant that I can't stop thinking about you—" Jacob paused, color rising in his cheeks. "That's not what I meant, either."

A smile tickled Kate's lips. She hadn't seen Jacob Dawson lose his composure once since meeting him, and she rather enjoyed it now. "It's okay."

Jacob shook his head and laughed uncomfortably. "I should stop talking now."

Kate nibbled her bottom lip to try to stop her smile. "And I should get into the sanctuary."

She started down the hall again, but stopped when Jacob called out to her.

"I'm happy you decided to come, Kate."

For some reason, his words filled her with incredible joy, and she turned to nod at him. "So am I."

Jacob's smile was welcoming, but it was also very attractive, a quality Kate both appreciated and wanted to ignore. It hadn't been easy, especially being on stage, but she had managed to avoid a romantic relationship since her high school boyfriend left her pregnant and afraid.

There hadn't been room in her life, or space in her heart, to let someone in again.

Kate turned back toward the hallway and took another steadying breath. A simple attraction was nothing to worry about. She'd denied the feelings for other men before, and she could do it again.

There were more important things to worry about.

The church lobby hummed with conversation as Jacob stood near the door, greeting people as they left the sanctuary after the service.

"I really enjoyed your sermon, Pastor," Ed Warren said, as he shook Jacob's hand.

"Thank you." Jacob nodded at Ed's compliment, doubting the authenticity of the comment.

Jacob was rarely as nervous delivering a sermon as he had been today. Kate's presence at the back of the sanctuary had tripped him up more than once. She had watched him so closely, as if hanging on his every word, making him overly self-conscious, a feeling he didn't get often. Her attention, coupled with the way he'd embarrassed himself moments before stepping up to the pulpit, had made him thankful the sermon was finally over.

He continued to shake people's hands as they left the church, aware of Kate standing near the sanctuary door, surrounded by several of the church ladies. She hadn't made it far out the door before they swarmed her.

"Will you excuse me?" Jacob asked one of his congregants as he stepped away. He loved and appreciated the older women who served the church, but they could be overwhelming at times.

Moving toward Kate, Jacob couldn't help but admire her poise and grace. It was obvious she was used to attention, and the closer he came to her, the more he doubted she needed him to interfere. He was about to turn away when she glanced up and noticed him.

Her smile stopped him in his tracks.

"Pastor Jacob," Mrs. Caruthers said when she noticed whom Kate was smiling at. "We were just talking about you."

"Oh?" It took Jacob a moment to compose his thoughts, but then he smiled at Mrs. Caruthers, Mrs. Topper, Mrs. Anderson and Mrs. Evans. "I hope you had something nice to say."

The women laughed at his joke.

"They were just telling me that you asked them to organize meals for the boys and me this week." Kate's eyes sparkled with appreciation when she spoke to him. "That's very nice, but I wouldn't want to impose."

"It's no imposition." Mrs. Caruthers put her

hand on Kate's. "And we won't take no for an answer. I've already created a sign-up sheet and it's full this week and next. You won't have to worry about making supper while you settle in."

"I'm making my famous tater-tot hot dish," Mrs. Anderson said, "with lime Jell-O for dessert. You can't say no to my lime Jell-O."

"And I'm bringing goulash—have you ever had goulash, my dear?" Mrs. Topper asked Kate.

Kate shook her head. "I'm afraid I haven't."

"I'll be sure to include my recipe, then." Mrs. Topper nodded. "I don't use store-bought marinara like some others do."

The lobby had grown warm as people stood around chatting. Sunlight poured through the stained glass windows, sending colorful glints across the room and resting on Kate's blond hair. He wondered if the stage lights made her silky hair look as beautiful as the stained glass.

"We were just telling Kate about the hayride and bonfire," Mrs. Caruthers said, with a knowing gleam in her eyes. "It's for the single people in our congregation."

"And we thought it would be a wonderful way for Kate to meet the other young people," Mrs. Topper added quickly.

The church ladies nodded enthusiastically.

"And since you live right across the street—"

Mrs. Anderson took Jacob's arm into her own, tugging him toward Kate's side "—we thought it only made sense for you to escort Miss LeClair to the event."

Jacob wanted to groan. It hadn't taken them long to play matchmaker.

"You're single," Mrs. Caruthers said. "Kate is single."

As if he weren't already painfully aware of this fact.

"It only makes sense," Mrs. Topper concluded. "It's a shame to see two young, attractive, kind people all alone."

"I'm not alone," Jacob reminded the well-meaning women. "My life is very full raising Maggie and shepherding this church community."

"But don't you have room for a little romance?" Mrs. Anderson winked at Jacob and nodded, as if she knew something he didn't. "Life is always better when you're in love—isn't that right, Miss LeClair?"

Kate's cheeks turned pink, and she didn't meet Jacob's gaze. "I wouldn't know."

"What?" all four church ladies said at once, their voices drawing attention from the others in the room.

"You've never been in love?" Mrs. Evans

shook her head. "How can that be? You're gorgeous!"

"Well—" Kate lowered her eyelashes in embarrassment "—I don't believe looks are a requirement for finding love."

Compassion tightened Jacob's stomach and he gently placed his hand under Kate's elbow. "I bet those boys are eager to see you again. I'll walk you to the nursery. I'm sure Maggie isn't too far away from them."

Kate glanced up at Jacob with appreciation in her gaze. "Thank you."

"It was nice to meet you," Mrs. Caruthers said. "You two be sure to work out the details for the hayride and bonfire."

"If you don't," Mrs. Evans warned, "we will."

The women grouped together into a tight knot, speaking quickly among themselves as Jacob led Kate away.

"Sorry about that," he said, letting go of her elbow and putting a little space between them. "I should have warned you."

"It's okay." She lifted a shoulder. "I've gotten a little used to unwanted attention over the years."

"You shouldn't have to deal with it at church, though." He was amazed at how much he had wanted her to like Timber Falls Community Church.

"Really," she said. "I don't mind."

"They're notorious matchmakers," he continued. "Unfortunately, they're relentless and won't leave us alone until we're happily matched."

"To each other?"

Jacob purposely didn't meet her stunning gaze at that moment, knowing it would only make him more uncomfortable. "Not necessarily."

Kate sighed. "Romance is the last thing on my mind right now."

His disappointment took him by surprise. "I'd hate for their interference to keep you away from church. Even if you're only going to be in town for a little while, I'd love to see you here as much as possible."

She glanced up at him and nodded. "I really enjoyed being here. Everyone is so welcoming—and your sermon was exactly what I needed to hear."

"Really?" Her compliment meant more to him than it should. "I was afraid I wasn't making sense."

"I was completely engaged the entire time."

"I'm happy to hear it."

She clasped her hands behind her back. "I'm already looking forward to next Sunday."

His steps felt lighter at her praise. "I am, too."

"Pastor?"

Jacob and Kate stopped on their way down the hallway and turned at the sound of a man's voice.

Rick Johnson strode toward them, his comb-over fluttering with each step.

Another inward groan wanted to escape, but Jacob put a smile on his face and squared his shoulders. The man was relentless and would no doubt pester Kate to sell her house.

At this rate, Kate would never return to the church.

"You must be Miss LeClair." Rick extended his large hand toward Kate and engulfed her smaller one in his grasp.

"Kate, this is our head elder, Rick Johnson."

"It's nice to meet you," Kate said.

Rick looked Kate over from head to toe, appreciation gleaming from his eyes. "And you."

Jacob didn't like the way Rick looked at her. "Miss LeClair was just about to go to the nursery to get—"

"I'm happy I caught you, then," Rick said to Kate, ignoring Jacob. "I wanted to talk to you about Tabby and Adam's house."

Kate glanced briefly at Jacob. "I heard the church has been trying to buy the house."

"Ah, good." Rick crossed his arms and slipped his hands under his armpits. "I see Pastor Jacob has already discussed our plans with you."

"I told Miss LeClair that we're interested in purchasing the house," Jacob said quickly, "but I understand that she's had a lot happen in the past few days and we're in no hurry to have an answer."

"You might not be in a hurry," Rick said with a scowl, "but the rest of us are." He turned his full attention back to Kate. "What does a pretty little thing like you need with a big old house like that?"

Kate's eyebrows came together.

"Miss LeClair's great-grandparents built the house." Jacob wished he could whisk Kate away from the distasteful man.

"Who cares who built it?" Rick asked. "We need the space for our new school. What's more important, a house or a school that can teach countless kids?"

The guilt and shame aimed at Kate made anger pulse under Jacob's skin. One of the hardest parts of his job was keeping the peace while standing up to the bullies. "I think we can all agree that a home and a school are equally important."

"Can we?" Rick shook his head. "I'd like your answer sooner than later, Miss LeClair. We have plans to make and we need to get moving."

"The children are waiting for us," Jacob said to Rick. "If you'll excuse us?"

Jacob put his hand under Kate's elbow again and led her away from Rick. He ran his free hand through his hair, and when they were far enough away, he said, "I'm sorry about that."

"It's okay."

"Rick was out of line."

"I know what it's like to have a dream and be faced with insurmountable obstacles."

Her grace and understanding put him to shame, and his admiration for her continued to grow. "Don't feel pressured to make a decision."

"I won't."

They came to the nursery door and Jacob asked, "Do you need some help getting the boys home?"

Kate took a deep breath and shook her head. "Thanks, but I think I can manage."

"If you need anything, don't forget to call."

She met his gaze and her face softened. "Thank you, Jacob. I appreciate your kindness."

He grinned—and continued to grin for the rest of the afternoon.

Chapter Five

Dark clouds sat low in the sky as Kate stepped out the front door in her robe and slippers. A cool nip in the air made her shiver as she held her steaming coffee cup in one hand and ran her other over her disheveled hair. It was the first morning she'd woken up before the triplets and she was pleasantly surprised at how good it felt to be up so early. The day before, she had noticed the newspapers piling up in the front yard and now she walked down the steps to pick up the newest addition on the sidewalk.

A handful of children waited at the corner as a yellow school bus came to a stop. Its red lights flashed and a stop sign popped out the side as the driver opened the door.

One of the little boys waved at Kate right before he got on the bus and she waved back.

Kate held the newspaper to her chest and inhaled the refreshing aroma of coffee. Timber Falls was every bit as charming as she remembered, and then some. As a child, she hadn't valued a good school, a good church or a good neighbor.

Her gaze landed on the beautiful blue Victorian home across the road and a smile tilted her lips. She'd felt bad for Jacob yesterday when the church ladies and the head elder had pressured her. It was obvious Jacob was uncomfortable with their behavior, but Kate knew they all meant well. Instead of turning her off the church, as she was certain Jacob worried, it had actually endeared her to it more. The people in Timber Falls cared deeply about each other, and it was that care that had prompted them to approach her.

It was an interesting part of small-town life, which she found she enjoyed very much.

A charcoal-gray Chevy Impala turned down Third Street and Kate's heart rate picked up a tick. She didn't want Jacob to catch her in her robe and slippers, so she turned toward the house. But a flash of red on the white picket fence caused her to pause.

Frowning, Kate walked over the leaf-strewn front lawn and inspected the fence facing the back of the church.

Someone had taken red spray paint and went

up and down the length of the fence in two wide streaks.

Who would do such a thing?

She glanced around the yard to see if there was any other vandalism and her gaze landed on the small brick barn that served as her garage. One of the old leaded windows had been broken.

"Kate?" Jacob stepped out of his car, which was now in the church parking lot. "What happened?"

"I don't know." She walked through the open gate to get a better look at the other side of the fence. "It looks like someone had fun at my expense last night."

Jacob strode toward her, a frown on his face. He wore a pair of black slacks, with a long dark coat. His shoes were shining and his hair perfectly combed. He looked like he was just coming from—or just going to—somewhere important. He shook his head in confusion as he inspected the damage. "Who would do something like this?"

She'd seen her fair share of vandalism in Chicago and New York and it didn't shock her as much as it seemed to shock the pastor. "You don't have vandalism in Timber Falls?" She couldn't help but smile at his astonishment.

"Of course we do, but it's usually not in this neighborhood."

Kate shrugged. "It was probably a group of bored kids."

"They broke your window, too." He walked toward the garage, continuing to shake his head. "Did they steal anything?"

"I don't know." She followed him toward the broken window, but he put his hand out to stop her.

"You shouldn't go near the glass in your slippers."

For the first time, Kate remembered she was still in her pajamas and heat filled her cheeks. She must look a fright—especially next to his polished appearance.

"I'll take a look around and clean up the glass," Jacob offered. "Why don't you call the police to file a report?"

"For a little spray paint and broken glass?"

"It's always good to have documentation—in case this continues." He bent to start picking up the shards of glass. "Although, I have a feeling this was a single incident."

"Wait until I get a garbage can for the—"

"Ow." He dropped the shard of glass he was holding and inspected his finger.

"Did you cut yourself?"

"It's nothing."

Kate went to his side and knelt in the lawn. She set down the newspaper and her cup of coffee, the smell of fallen leaves mingling with Jacob's cologne. "Let me see." She didn't wait for him to show her but reached for his hand.

Their shoulders brushed, and when she touched his hand, a tingle of awareness raced up her arm.

"It's just a little cut," he said, trying to pull away, his voice low. "I'm fine."

"Is the glass still in there?"

"No." He was so close to her, she could feel his warm breath on her cheek. "It was a large piece that cut me."

It really wasn't that big of a cut, but she would feel better if it was taken care of. "Let's go inside and wash it, and then I'll get a bandage for you."

"I'll be okay." He gently pulled his hand away but didn't leave his spot on the lawn. "Thanks for your concern, though."

She finally looked in his direction and found he was much closer than she'd realized. "A-are you sure?"

Jacob smiled, his dimples deep and charming.

"You spend all your time taking care of everyone else," she said quietly. "It's okay to take a little help now and again."

He studied her for a heartbeat and then glanced at her pajamas. "Aren't you cold?"

She couldn't be any warmer, even if she'd been in a thick winter coat. "I'm fine."

They didn't speak for a moment and Kate finally stood. "I'll go get that garbage can and call the police."

She started to walk away.

"Don't forget your coffee," he called out to her.

"Have you had any today?" she asked.

He stood and lifted the mug, shaking his head.

"Have mine." She tilted her head in the direction of the kitchen. "I'll get another cup for myself."

"Are you sure?"

She nodded. "Coffee is always better when you can share it with a friend."

"I couldn't agree more."

Kate could feel his gaze as she walked toward the house. She was used to people watching her on stage, and had grown almost numb to men's appreciative stares, but when she glanced back at Jacob, his warm gaze lit a spark of pleasure in her stomach.

Stepping inside the kitchen, Kate closed the door. Jacob went back to work cleaning up the glass and she had the chance to watch him, un-hindered for a moment.

She'd never met a man like him. He was both strong and manly, yet he didn't hesitate to stoop low and help where needed. He was compassionate, humble and funny—but more than that, he was just a good man. It made her wonder more and more about the woman who had captured this man's heart. What kind of person had Laura been? Had she been just as amazing as him? Just as good and pure and humble?

Kate pulled her robe closer to her body and felt the shiver run up the length of her spine. No matter how hard she tried, Kate could never be anything like Jacob. She was stained and soiled, and nothing she could do would change that fact.

Jacob hadn't been able to focus well since seeing the vandalism at Kate's earlier in the day, but he managed to get most of his work done. He had performed a small funeral at a nursing home in the morning and then spent a few hours outlining the sermon he planned to give on Sunday. It was part of a new series on the life of the prophet Samuel. In the afternoon, he had visited Mrs. Meacham in the hospital, as well as two other elderly members of their church community. While he was out, he had attended a monthly pastoral meeting with the other ministers in Timber Falls, and then he'd met for coffee with a couple he was counseling who planned to get married at the end of next month.

It had been a busy day, but Jacob was thankful it was over and he could pick Maggie up from Kate's. He left the church and didn't bother to get into his car, but walked across the road to his house. There, he changed into a pair of worn blue jeans and a faded sweatshirt and then grabbed several tools out of his garage. It was past time to clean up Kate's lawn, and what better time to do it than now?

With his rake, shovel and clippers in the wheelbarrow, Jacob crossed the street again and set the wheelbarrow just inside the fence. He'd have to fix the garage window and paint over the red spray paint, too, but for now he'd focus his energy on the yard.

Leaving the wheelbarrow, he walked around the house, went to the kitchen door and knocked. He waited for several minutes, but no one came to the door, so he turned the knob and found it was unlocked.

"Hello?" He poked his head into the kitchen. "Kate? Maggie?"

The sound of singing met his ears. The sweet

notes of "Baby Mine" echoed through the house and made him pause.

Was that Kate?

He'd never heard anything more pure or lovely in his life and couldn't stop himself from following the sound through the empty kitchen, down the front hall and up the stairs. The song spilled from the room at the back of the house where the boys slept.

Jacob walked through the hallway and stopped just outside the bedroom door. Kate sat in a gliding chair, one of the boys in her arms, while the other two lay in their cribs. Maggie sat cross-legged on a thick rug on the floor, her gaze fully captured by Kate.

The shades were drawn, but light seeped in around the cracks, offering just enough illumination for Jacob to see Kate's face as she looked down at the baby in her arms. "Baby mine, don't you cry," she sang, as she stroked his cheek. "Baby mine, dry your eyes. Rest your head close to my heart, never to part, baby of mine."

Her words faded away, but she kept rocking and gazing down at the sleeping boy in her arms. Maggie didn't move, which surprised Jacob, since his daughter rarely sat still.

Finally, Kate stood and gently laid the baby

boy in his crib, then she motioned for Maggie to follow her.

It was then that Kate noticed Jacob standing in the hallway, just outside the room.

"Daddy!" Maggie said and both Jacob and Kate jumped to quiet her.

Maggie slapped her hand over her mouth while Kate tiptoed over and looked into the cribs.

"Shh," Jacob said, walking Maggie farther away from the boys' bedroom.

"Sorry," Maggie whispered.

Kate stepped out of the room and quietly closed the door behind her. "It's okay," she said in her own whisper. "They're still napping."

Jacob motioned down the stairs and Kate nodded.

When they all stood in the foyer, Jacob finally let out the breath he was holding. "You sing beautifully, Kate."

"Thank you."

"She's an actress, Daddy." Maggie shook her head, clearly exasperated by his lack of memory. "She has to sing pretty."

Kate winked at the little girl.

"Would you consider leading worship at church sometime?" Jacob asked, unable to keep the question to himself. "As you might have guessed, we're in need of a female vocalist."

A funny look came over Kate's face and she dropped her gaze.

Heat gathered under Jacob's collar and he was immediately embarrassed he'd asked. What had made him think that a Broadway star would want to sing in his humble little church? She probably had an acting agent and a contract that prevented her from singing publicly without permission from her producer. Even if she agreed to sing, she'd probably need to charge him an astronomical fee.

"I'm sorry," he said quickly. "I shouldn't have asked. You probably have a clause in your contract—"

"No." She shook her head. "It's not that."

Maggie looked up expectantly at Kate, admiration shining in her big blue eyes. "Could I sing with you, Kate?"

"Maybe now's not the time to ask." Jacob put a hand on his daughter's shoulder.

"It's okay," Kate said. "I don't mind you asking." Her cheeks grew pink. "I just don't think I'm the right person to sing for your church."

"I understand." It was probably an embarrassment for him to even ask her. "We probably couldn't afford you, anyway."

"I wouldn't ask you to pay me." Kate finally looked up at Jacob. "It's not that—I just don't think I'm the right person to sing in church, that's all."

What did she mean by that? Why wouldn't she be the right person?

"In other news," Kate said abruptly, grinning at Maggie. "Your daughter is one talented girl."

Jacob was ready to change the subject, too. "I've always suspected as much," he said.

"She offered to help me go through some of Tabby and Adam's things." Kate touched Maggie's ponytail affectionately. "And she's very organized."

"I wonder why her organizational skills don't work in her bedroom." Jacob put his hand up to his chin and frowned.

"Oh, Daddy," Maggie said playfully.

"We started in the basement right after she came home from school and worked until it was time to put the boys down for their afternoon nap."

"And Kate gave me some dolls." Maggie's eyes shined bright. "They're *very* old."

"Maybe they're valuable," Jacob said to Kate. "Are you sure it's okay?"

"I am just happy they will be loved." Kate put her hands together. "And now that the boys are sleeping, I should head back down there and keep working."

"May I stay and help?" Maggie asked Jacob.

"I was planning to do a fall cleanup in the yard." Jacob addressed Kate. "Do you mind if Maggie hangs out with you a bit longer?"

"Of course not, but you shouldn't have to clean the yard."

"It's no bother. The forecast says snow, so we should get it done."

"I can put off organizing for now," Kate offered. "How about I come outside and help you in the yard instead?"

Jacob couldn't deny the pleasure he felt at that prospect. "I'd like that."

"So would I." Kate was already wearing some jeans and an older Harvard sweatshirt. "Let me grab the boys' monitor and I'll join you in a minute."

"Sounds good." Jacob led Maggie out the front door and into the yard.

"I like Kate," Maggie said, as she turned to look up at Jacob.

"I like her, too." Jacob went to the wheelbarrow and pulled out a pair of work gloves.

"She's nice," Maggie added.

Jacob only smiled.

Maggie walked up to the wheelbarrow and leaned against it. "Can you marry her, Daddy?"

"What?" Jacob stopped putting on his gloves. His daughter had never once asked him that before.

"Can you marry her?" Maggie asked matter-of-factly. "Then she can be my mommy and the triplets can be my little brothers."

"It's not as easy as that, Mags."

"Why not?" Her genuine question tugged at his heart.

He sighed. "Because life is hardly ever that simple."

"Why? You said you like her."

"I like a lot of people, but that doesn't mean I want to marry them."

"Don't you want to marry Kate?"

"Now is not the time or place to discuss this. What if Kate heard you?"

"I already asked her."

Jacob stared at his daughter, his pulse picking up speed. "You did?"

"Yes." Maggie grabbed the handle of the rake and started to play with it.

"What did she say?"

Maggie shrugged and pulled on the handle, making the rake fall out of the wheelbarrow and onto the grass. She bent over to pick it up. "She said she can't get married now." His daughter's disappointment was keen. "But you can change her mind, can't you, Daddy?"

Kate chose that moment to step outside, a wrinkle in her brow.

It was the perfect opportunity to redirect his

daughter's attention. "Maggie, can you pick up the water hose so we can rake?"

"Sure!" Maggie skipped off to do his bidding and Jacob was able to turn his attention on Kate.

"Is everything okay?" he asked.

"I just received a message from the Family Medical Center. Apparently, the boys missed their eighteen-month well-baby check-up this afternoon. The clinic had a cancellation for tomorrow and asked if I could take the boys in the morning."

Jacob watched her, waiting for more of an explanation, but she didn't give one. "Why do you look so upset?"

Anxiety radiated from her eyes. "I've only taken them to church—which is next door. It terrifies me to think about getting them in the minivan and taking them out in public—to a doctor's appointment, no less."

"I'd be happy to help you." He leaned on the rake. "I've been taking Maggie to her appointments since she was about their age. I think we could manage."

"I couldn't ask you to do that. You've already done far too much for me."

"Kate, it's my job." But more than that, he wanted to help her—wanted any excuse he could find to spend time with her.

She frowned, uncertainty in the depths of her

beautiful eyes. "Are you sure you don't have something more important to do?"

He would have to cancel his appointment with a realtor who was helping the church look for possible locations for a school, but it would be easy enough to reschedule. "I'm sure."

Something in her face told him she didn't believe him, but he didn't care. "I'll even come by early and help you get them ready."

Kate studied him for a moment and then let out the breath she'd been holding. "Thank you. You don't know how much I appreciate your offer."

"My pleasure." An awkward pause filled the air between them, so he said, "Should we get started on the lawn?"

Kate nodded and set the monitor on the steps.

With a smile, Jacob realized he had never looked forward to cleaning a lawn more than he did today.

Chapter Six

It was fun to laugh and tease with Jacob and Maggie as the three of them worked on the front yard. Kate still had a hard time thinking of the house as hers, but there was a small part of her that had always thought of it as home, even though she'd only spent one week there as a child. Every time she and her mother were forced to leave one bad apartment to find the next, she had taken comfort in knowing that the charming house in Timber Falls was solid and unmovable.

"What other parts have you played on stage?" Jacob asked Kate as he raked the leaves into a pile near the walk.

Kate had found a rake in her garage and was raking another pile nearby. They hadn't made as much progress as they probably could have, had they not spent so much time talking.

"I can't even count all the plays I've been in," Kate acknowledged. "I started when I was about Maggie's age."

"I've been in two plays." Maggie perked up from where she was playing in a pile of leaves on the other side of the yard. "*Robin Hood* and *Cinderella*."

"I was in both of those plays, too," Kate told the little girl. "Several times, in fact."

"What made you want to pursue the stage?" Jacob leaned on his rake. "It's such a fascinating career choice."

Kate continued to rake for a moment as she tried to articulate her answer. Usually, she gave a generic response to that question, but she felt safer talking to Jacob about her real reasons. "When I was little, it was a lot more fun to pretend I was someone other than Kate LeClair. There were no limitations to who I could be and what I could do if I was playing someone else on stage."

Jacob was quiet for a moment as he nodded reflectively. "Do you find that's still the case?"

She had never asked herself that question before, and found the answer surprised her. "No. Now that I'm an adult and, for the most part, I can control who I am and where I go, I don't need the stage to escape." She finished her corner of the yard and moved to the next section.

"Now I act because it's become so much a part of who I am I cannot imagine doing anything else."

That is, until she came back to Timber Falls. For the first time in her life, she started to wonder what it would be like to stay in one home and raise a family.

Four cars turned down Third Street, one after the other, and came to a stop near the front curb.

A smile tilted Kate's lips as four older women opened their doors in almost perfect unison and stepped out.

"It's the church ladies," Maggie said with a groan. "And it's not even Sunday."

Jacob turned to his daughter and frowned while he shook his head to silence her.

"Yoo-hoo!" Mrs. Caruthers called out as she waved. "Pastor, could you come and help us haul in supper?"

"Haul in supper?" Kate's eyes grew wide.

"We've all brought you a little something for the meal," Mrs. Topper said to Kate. "I made the bread, Mrs. Anderson made the tater-tot hot dish, Mrs. Caruthers made a salad and Mrs. Evans made the strawberry-pretzel dessert. But don't you worry, you'll get another meal tomorrow. I plan to bring you goulash, remember?"

"I couldn't possibly eat all that food in one

day," Kate protested. "Please don't feel obligated to make me another meal tomorrow."

"We made enough for you, the boys, Pastor and Maggie." Mrs. Caruthers opened her passenger door and pulled out a basket. "Now you can invite Pastor to stay for supper."

The women giggled and smiled at one another, as if they had concocted a scheme—and perhaps they had.

"Now, where should we put this, dear?" Mrs. Anderson asked as she held a large basket.

Kate set her rake against the wheelbarrow and motioned for them to follow her. "In the kitchen."

She led the way, all four ladies, as well as Jacob and Maggie, following close behind.

Even outside, she couldn't deny that the food smelled amazing. She had never had tater-tot hot dish, and wasn't even sure what it was, but if it tasted as good as it smelled, she'd love it.

Opening the door, she allowed everyone to enter her kitchen ahead of her. Dishes were still in the sink from breakfast and lunch, and dried macaroni and cheese was stuck to the boys' high chairs. One of them had thrown their applesauce across the room, and it was still dripping down the wall.

Mortification engulfed her unexpectedly as the women stood around and surveyed the room.

"My, my," Mrs. Evans said. "It looks like you've been…busy."

Jacob set one of the baskets down on the table. "Kate has done an amazing job with the boys," he said. "And did you know she volunteers to watch Maggie after school while Mrs. Meacham recovers?"

"Oh." Mrs. Caruthers nodded. "How nice of you, Miss LeClair."

Kate's cheeks flushed hot and she quickly picked up the gallon of milk and shoved it into the fridge. "Thank you for the meal. It will free me up to get some cleaning done this evening."

"Yes, well." Mrs. Topper set down her basket and offered a smile. "That will be nice."

"Have you two worked out the details for the hayride and bonfire?" Mrs. Caruthers asked suddenly.

Kate met Jacob's gaze.

"We've been a little preoccupied," Jacob supplied. "Kate had some vandalism on her property overnight."

"Yes, we heard." Mrs. Anderson clucked her tongue as she shook her head. "But surely you've had enough time to discuss the hayride."

"What hayride, Daddy?" Maggie asked.

Jacob filled his chest with air and then let it out slowly. He was a patient man.

"There's a hayride and bonfire at the Carsons' farm this weekend."

"May I go?"

"It's only for adults, sweetheart."

"Then you'll take Kate?" Maggie asked.

Jacob didn't answer immediately, and Kate wanted to spare him from the embarrassment. "I have the boys to look after—"

"It's already been taken care of," Mrs. Topper said in a singsong voice. "The four of us have volunteered to come here and watch the boys and Maggie." She smiled demurely. "So you have no excuses."

Jacob looked at Kate, something akin to empathy on his face. "Did you want to go to the hayride and bonfire, Kate?"

Kate had never been to one—and secretly, she had always wanted to go. There had been no opportunities for things like that when she was growing up. But she didn't want to inconvenience Jacob, either.

"I can see it in her face," Mrs. Evans said. "She wants to go."

Smiling, and trying to hide the longing in her face, she nodded at Jacob. "I wouldn't mind going."

A smile lifted Jacob's mouth and his eyes filled with pleasure.

"Then it's settled." Mrs. Evans clapped her hands. "Pastor, you'll take Kate."

Maggie clapped, too, and looked just as pleased as the older women.

"Well." Mrs. Caruthers's face glowed. "I think our work here is done. We should be off."

The women left Kate's kitchen just as quickly as they'd arrived.

Kate didn't move as she faced Jacob, the quiet left in the church ladies' wake almost deafening.

"I told you they wouldn't let us alone until they had their way." Jacob shook his head, the smile still on his face.

Laughter started to bubble up in Kate's chest until it spilled over. "I've never experienced anything like them."

"They mean well." Jacob frowned. "I think."

Maggie watched Jacob and Kate with a raised eyebrow.

"It would almost be easier to pretend we're dating," Kate said with more laughter. "They just might leave us alone then."

Jacob's face grew serious. "That's actually a really good idea."

Kate's laughter quieted as she studied Jacob. "Do you think it would work?"

He shrugged. "It couldn't hurt."

"Isn't that a lie, Daddy?" Maggie crossed her arms and frowned.

"It's more like acting," Kate told the girl. "Just like being on a stage. We'll play the part of a dating couple."

Maggie continued to frown, but Kate could tell she was mulling over the idea.

"I'm game, if you are," Jacob said slowly.

Kate shrugged, the laughter still making her feel carefree. "Let's give it a shot."

"Can we eat first?" Maggie asked impatiently. "I'm hungry."

Kate and Jacob started to laugh again, and Kate couldn't deny how good it felt.

If it was this easy and this much fun to hang out with Jacob and Maggie, Kate would have no trouble pretending to date the handsome pastor.

It was already dark by the time Jacob walked Maggie across the street to their home that evening. The air was cold and he could see his breath. His weather app had sent an alert that the first snow was expected overnight. They probably wouldn't get more than a dusting, but he felt better about having Kate's yard cleaned and ready for winter.

Behind him, several lights still glowed in Kate's house, a remnant of their time together. After supper, they had played with the boys in the toy room and then helped Kate put them to bed.

Maggie yawned and reached for Jacob's hand

as they walked up the stairs to the large wrap-around porch. Their footsteps tapped against the wood floor until they came to the welcome mat.

"It's been a long day for you." Jacob lifted his little girl into his arms as he opened their front door. She snuggled into him, resting her head on his shoulder.

"Thank you for all your help at Kate's today," he told her.

Maggie wrapped her arms around Jacob's neck and sighed contentedly. "I like her."

Jacob wasn't about to start that conversation again.

He flipped on the foyer light, illuminating the dark oak staircase, the Victorian floral wallpaper and the antique furniture the church had furnished with the house. It had been move-in ready when he and Maggie came to Timber Falls, making him feel like he had stepped back in time. He'd been told the house had been built for the first pastor of Timber Falls Community Church and the man had been blessed with an enormous family. Original leaded windows, with stained glass embellishments, heavy light fixtures with intricate designs and thick oriental rugs with wear patterns graced the impeccable home. Even the sofa in the front parlor, and the dining room table just beyond, were original period pieces. He was almost afraid to let Maggie touch anything, so they spent most of their time in his study, which was the back parlor. There, he'd brought in his own couch, a flat-screen television and a rocking recliner. It was all the space the two of them needed.

"We'll skip your bath tonight, since you're so tired," he said to his daughter. "You can take one in the morning before school."

"Okay," she said in a sleepy voice.

He walked her up the wide curving staircase to the long hallway on the second floor. The house had five bedrooms upstairs alone, with two more under the eaves in the attic, and one off the kitchen, which he assumed was the maid's room at one point. His and Maggie's rooms were at the front of the house, close to the top of the stairs.

Flipping on Maggie's bedroom light, Jacob finally set his little girl on her own feet. "I'll come back in when you're in your pajamas and tuck you into bed."

"Okay, Daddy." She went to her armoire, since there was no closet in the room, and pulled open the bottom drawer where she kept her nightgowns.

Jacob went to his own bedroom and flipped on his light. The first thing that greeted him was the picture of Laura, which he kept on the fireplace mantel in the large room. It was the headshot she'd had taken right after college, just before they were married, when she had been accepted into medical school.

Her magnificent blue eyes shined, just like Maggie's did, and her brown hair, which had a natural curl, was cut just above her shoulders. She had been so happy then, so carefree and full of the possibilities that awaited them.

Tossing his coat across the wingback chair, Jacob walked over to the picture and lifted it off the mantel. He and Laura had been together since their first day of college. They'd met at orientation, ending up beside each other in the large auditorium. They were married four years later, before she started medical school and he started his seminary program. Three years after that, when he'd finished his studies and been hired at his first church, they moved to a small town an hour away from her school. She agreed to the commute, though it wasn't easy.

He'd loved his new job, but had immediately felt the pressure to start a family. The other pastor at the church had a wife and small children, and their ministry was done as a family unit. Jacob often felt alone with Laura working and going to school. They hardly saw each other and it started to affect their relationship. Jacob had made matters worse by pressuring Laura to start a family. He didn't want to be an old father—and he felt it would be better for his church standing if they had children.

A year later, when Laura graduated from medical school, before starting her residency program, she had finally consented. It didn't take them long to conceive Maggie.

Jacob sighed and sat on the wingback chair, shaking his head. Why had he been so selfish? Why couldn't he have let the matter drop?

Within two months of learning about the baby, Laura was diagnosed with skin cancer. They removed the spot, but later discovered the cancer had spread. Because of her pregnancy, they were unable to treat her with radiation or chemotherapy. By the time Maggie was born, it was too late. They fought hard, but Laura died eighteen months later.

Jacob closed his eyes and asked God to forgive him for the hundredth time.

"Daddy?" Maggie called from the next room. "I'm ready!"

A smile tilted Jacob's lips as he stood and replaced Laura's picture. One of his mentors had once told Jacob that out of the ashes of the tragedy, God had provided Jacob with his beautiful daughter. If Laura hadn't become pregnant when she did, then Jacob would not have Maggie. The little girl had been a healing balm to his soul and he thanked God for her every day.

His daughter, who had been almost asleep when they got home, was now sitting on her bed, wide-awake, with her favorite stuffed bunny in her arms.

"Daddy, can I see Kate sing on stage?"

He pulled her covers back and she climbed under them.

"She's not acting right now."

"I know." She held Bunny up for Jacob to kiss, which he did. "I mean on YouTube."

"YouTube?" He frowned and sat on the bed beside her, tucking the thick quilt in around her.

"She told me today that she's on YouTube." Maggie blinked expectantly at him.

"Do you know what YouTube is?"

"Nope. But can I watch it?"

Jacob smiled. "I suppose—but not tonight. It's too late."

"Okay." Maggie scooted down until her head was on her pillow. "After my bath tomorrow."

Nodding, Jacob ran his hand over Maggie's forehead, removing some of the stray tendrils that slipped over her face. "Are you ready for our prayers?"

She nodded and pulled her hand out from under the covers to grab hold of his. It was small and delicate and he held it gently. She closed her eyes, a contented smile on her tiny lips.

Jacob admired her for a heartbeat, marveling that she looked more and more like Laura every day.

"Lord, we thank You for today," he began. "We thank You for this warm home, full bellies and our good health. We thank You for our friends and family—"

"Especially Kate," Maggie added quickly.

"And for our work." Jacob didn't skip a beat, used to his daughter interjecting her own prayers—something he'd always encouraged her to do. "We ask that You forgive us for our sins and help us to do better tomorrow—"

"Please forgive me for sticking my tongue out at Heather today."

"We pray for protection, rest and the opportunity to bless those around us. In Your name, we pray. Amen."

"Amen." Maggie opened her eyes, but she didn't let go of Jacob's hand. "I'm happy you're a pastor—even if we have church ladies."

A smile tickled Jacob's lips. "And why's that?"

She blinked at him, as if the answer should be obvious. "Because then you and Jesus can be friends."

"Jesus can be anyone's friend, Mags. Not just a pastor's. He's your friend, too. Did you know that?"

Maggie shook her head.

"It's true. You can talk to Him whenever you want. You don't have to wait for me to talk to Him."

"Really?"

Jacob nodded.

"Can He be Kate's friend, too?"

"Of course He can."

"Good!" She nuzzled into her pillow and closed her eyes, a yawn on her lips. "I'll tell her tomorrow."

Jacob walked to the door, loving the simplicity of his daughter's heart. "Good night, Mags."

"Good night, Daddy."

He flipped off the light and closed the door. Standing in the dark hallway, he put his hands in his pockets and just stood for a moment. The wind picked up outside, rattling the old windows and putting a chill in the drafty house.

Just ahead of him, at the stairway window, the bare branches swayed in the wind and the first snowflakes brushed against the glass.

He walked down the hallway to the back stairs and flipped on the light to adjust the thermostat. It seemed like a waste to heat the whole house when it was just the two of them.

Almost immediately, the old radiators started to hiss and clink as the system began to work.

Maggie wouldn't let the YouTube thing rest until Jacob showed it to her, and since their mornings were usually hectic already, he decided to go down the stairs to his office and search for Kate on the internet. At least then he'd have something to show Maggie in the morning.

The back stairs entered into the kitchen, so he flipped the light on in there and grabbed a glass of water before going through the swinging door and the narrow butler's pantry. His office was next to the dining room, so he walked around the long oak table and flipped on the switch in the back parlor.

His laptop waited for him on the desk where he'd been working on his sermon series the night before. Tapping the power button, the screen turned on almost immediately.

Taking a seat, he rolled the chair up to the desk and clicked a browser icon. In the search bar, he typed Kate LeClair. Within seconds, dozens of links appeared on the screen. Interviews, performances, her website—and even a fan page. Jacob's eyebrows rose as he read the links. He hadn't expected to find so much.

Where did he begin? He could be here for hours.

A YouTube link was the third option, so he clicked it.

The caption read *Kate LeClair at Detroit's Magnificent Fox Theatre as Fantine in the Broadway Tour of* Les Misérables.

There she stood in a long white gown, her dark blond hair in waves around her shoulders, on an empty stage with the spotlight on her. He hit Play and the orchestra music swelled as Kate began to sing "I Dreamed a Dream."

He sat completely transfixed as she sang with intense passion and conviction rolling off her in waves. He'd never heard something so beautiful or so heartbreaking in all his life. Even though he knew Kate, he couldn't help but picture her as the young Fantine she was portraying. Her performance was so believable there was a part of him that wondered if Kate could relate to the words she was singing. When the song came to an end, an immense applause erupted and the camera spanned over one of the largest theaters he'd ever seen. There had to be close to five thousand people clapping and cheering for her, many on their feet, though the show had not ended.

Jacob stared at the screen, shocked and speechless. He'd had no idea—and this was just one theater.

The side of the screen showed dozens of other performances by Kate, in several different shows. Instead of watching them, he went to Facebook and looked up her name. Her artist page popped up and his mouth slipped open when he saw forty-five thousand people followed her.

Forty-five *thousand*? That was four times the amount of people in Timber Falls.

Clicking Like, he scrolled down her page and saw the most recent post, dated four days ago when she was in Charleston. It was a live video, which had already been viewed over fifteen thousand times. It began to play.

"Sorry I haven't shared my live video for this stop on the tour yet," Kate spoke to the camera as it followed her around the back stage. "And since tonight is the last performance in Charleston, I thought I had better get to it!" She bumped into a crew member and giggled as she apologized. The man smiled at her and didn't bother to glance at the camera. "The cast and crew are so used to my videos," she teased, "they don't even say hi anymore."

The man in the video laughed and then waved at the camera. "Hi," he said.

She squeezed his arm and shook her head. "Anything can happen in a live video—and I can't edit out my clumsiness." She continued onto the stage where the first scene was being set in place. "We're here in the amazing North Charleston Performing Arts Center where the twenty-three-hundred-seat theatre is sold out for tonight's performance." The camera spanned the empty theater, the lights low. "Tomorrow we're moving on to Memphis—"

"Kate!" A woman called out to Kate as she rushed onto the stage.

"It's one of my producers," Kate said when the camera landed back on her. "She's probably coming to tell me I left one of my props on the wrong table." Kate's smile was wide and carefree.

"Kate, we've been trying to find you," the producer said with concern in her voice, apparently not aware of the camera, either. "A social worker just called from Minnesota—your cousin has died."

The camera was still on Kate. Her eyes filled with shock and she shook her head in confusion. "What?"

Then the video went dead.

Over two thousand comments filled the post under the video, everyone offering their condolences and asking if Kate was doing okay. Jacob scrolled past them, reading a few as he went. Everyone wanted to know when Kate would rejoin the tour.

She hadn't yet responded.

Jacob leaned back in his chair. It creaked in protest as he crossed his arms and stared at the computer screen.

He'd had no idea. No clue that Kate LeClair was so famous or dearly loved by her fans.

He now had a better understanding of how difficult her decisions would be.

Chapter Seven

Somewhere in the background of Kate's morning, she remembered hearing her phone ding with a text message or two, but she still hadn't had time to even look at her phone.

"No, no," she said to Carter as she stepped over the gate into the boys' toy room where Aiken was wailing. "Don't pull your brother's hair."

Carter stood over his brother, who was sitting on the floor, a wad of Aiken's hair in his pudgy fist. Aiken held a toy train in his hands.

"My choo choo!" Carter yelled.

Kate took Carter's hand away from Aiken's hair and picked up the angry little boy. "Aiken has the choo choo," she said. "You can play with something else."

"Choo choo." Carter tried to nosedive out of Kate's hands to get the toy, but Kate had learned her lesson with him the first day and she was prepared for the attempt.

Bryce stood in the corner of the room, his thumb in his mouth, watching quietly.

"It's almost time to leave," Kate told Carter, who still struggled to get out of her arms. "Play with your basketball." She picked it up off the floor and put it in Carter's hands. It was the best distraction she had found and it worked. He threw it at the net and then wiggled to get out of her arms so he could do it again.

Aiken still sat on the floor, tears wetting his cheeks as he clutched the train.

Kate picked him up next and wiped his tears with the back of her sleeve. She kissed his head and nuzzled her face into his chest, making him giggle. "There you go, sweets."

There were still so many things she needed to get ready before taking the boys to their appointment. She had already dressed and fed them—and then changed Carter's outfit, because he had spilled grape juice down his shirt. She still needed to fill their backpack with extra diapers, a couple changes of clothes and some snacks.

The cell phone dinged again and Kate let out a long breath. Maybe it was important.

She went into the living room, assuming it was still where she'd left it the night before when she fell asleep watching *Call the Midwife*. It was sitting on the arm of the couch.

Picking it up, the screen turned on and she found five texts. Two were from her agent, one was from her producer and the other two were from her best friend, Peg, who was her hair-and-makeup artist for the show.

Kate sighed and sat on the couch. She'd have to deal with her life sooner rather than later.

Everyone wanted to know how she was doing and if she still planned to come back at the end of December. Her producer's text asked if she'd consider coming back any sooner. The understudy who had taken her place was not doing well and they were thinking about replacing her. It would be easier to have Kate return.

Bryce walked up to the gate situated between the toy room and the living room. His thumb was still in his mouth as he watched Kate with curiosity. His big blue eyes were so pure, so trusting, she couldn't help but smile.

"Mama?" he asked around his thumb.

She wondered how much the boys understood—especially Bryce who seemed to be the most sensitive of the triplets.

"It's okay," Kate told him, trying to hide the anxiety she felt about the weeks to come.

"Mama okay," he said.

She nodded. In a very short time, the boys

had stopped asking for their mama and had started to call Kate mama instead. She had wanted to correct them at first, but had chosen not to. They needed a mama, and right now, Kate was all they had.

It only took a couple seconds to respond to her producer that she couldn't possibly return to the show early. There were still so many things she needed to do…and decide.

She hit Send and then a knock at the front door shifted her attention.

It would probably be Jacob.

Kate ran her hand over her hair and tucked some of the stray pieces back into her messy bun. A quick perusal of her skinny jeans and blouse showed her that somehow Carter had splashed grape juice on her, too.

What did it matter? Even if she changed, she'd just get dirty again.

"Come in!" she called, as she walked into the foyer.

Jacob opened the door, but instead of his warm and welcoming smile, there was a bit of nerves hiding in his eyes. "Good morning, Kate."

"Good morning, Jacob."

He stepped into the foyer and she closed the door behind him.

Today, he wore dark blue jeans, a polo shirt and a navy-blue peacoat. His hair was a little ruffled from the wind, giving him a more casual look.

Jacob glanced at her and caught her staring. Her cheeks instantly grew warm and she looked away.

"I'm sorry I didn't get here sooner," he said. "I was up late last night and overslept this morning, and then Maggie had to have a bath and refused to leave the house before she could see you perform on YouTube." He spoke so quickly she almost didn't catch what he'd said. "So she was a bit late getting to school—and now I'm late getting here."

Kate just blinked. "I didn't notice you were late." She glanced at her phone and saw that they still had half an hour before they needed to be at the clinic.

"I wanted to get here earlier to help." He paused and studied her. "I had a chance to see you singing on stage." There was awe and a little incredulity in his voice. "I had no idea you were so amazing."

Embarrassment made her lower her eyes. "I wouldn't call it amazing."

"No, I'm serious." He shook his head. "You're simply stunning on stage. The way you connect with your audience is nothing short of brilliant." He laughed and this time he lowered his gaze to look at his hands. "I can't believe I asked you to sing at our humble little church."

"Your church is wonderful." It was her turn to gush. "The way you preach and care for your parishioners is nothing short of brilliant." She smiled when he shifted uncomfortably. "What I do is nowhere near as important as what you do, day after day. If anyone should get praise, it's you."

He finally looked up at her and met her gaze. His humility was so inspiring to her.

"I think it's safe to say that both of us are doing important work," he conceded. "And we're doing what God created us to do. Can there be anything better than that?"

One of the boys started to cry again.

"It sounds like that work is calling me now." Kate put her hand on Jacob's arm as she passed him. "This particular audience is never quite pleased with my performance."

Jacob laughed and followed her to the toy room. "It's not that they're not pleased—they simply want an encore."

"Night and day, around the clock." She stopped and admired the boys, amazed that she'd kept them safe and relatively happy for four days.

It took them almost thirty minutes to get the boys ready and buckled into the minivan. When Jacob offered to drive, Kate wholeheartedly agreed.

"Sorry we're going to be late," Jacob said, as

he pulled out of the garage. "Hopefully the doctor understands."

"I'm starting to realize that I need to add at least a half hour, if not longer, on to my schedule just to get these boys out the door."

They drove through Timber Falls and Kate enjoyed seeing some of the places she'd forgotten from her childhood. Ruby's Bistro, The Falls Movie Theater, the arts center and more.

"When we get to the clinic, I'll take out the stroller while you start to unbuckle the first boy," Jacob said. "Then you can put him in the stroller while I get the second, and when I'm putting the second one in the stroller, you can get out the third. Then I'll close all the doors and you can start pushing them into the building."

Kate couldn't hide her grin.

"What?" he asked.

"It sounds like we're going into battle."

His eyes shined with amusement. "Aren't we?"

The clinic parking lot was full when they arrived, but Jacob's plan went smoothly, and a few minutes later, Kate found herself sitting in the waiting room with Jacob at her side and the boys content in their stroller with graham crackers—for the time being.

One of the doors opened and Joy Asher stepped out. She waved when she saw Kate and immediately came over.

"Hey," she said to Kate and Jacob.

Kate was genuinely happy to see Joy. She'd only had a few minutes to chat with her at church the other day.

"I was just thinking about you," Joy said, taking a seat next to Kate.

"Is everything okay?" Kate glanced at the door Joy had just exited.

"Everything's fine. I was just here for a routine prenatal appointment." She rested her hand on her growing belly, her cheeks glowing. "Halfway there."

Memories of Kate's pregnancy seven years earlier rushed back at her unexpectedly. It had been the most thrilling—and most heart-wrenching—experience of her life. To know she had a baby growing in her but to also know that once she gave birth, she'd never see it again, had almost broken her heart in two. She'd never been the same, and whenever she saw another little girl about the age of her own, it made her heart break all over again—until she met Maggie. The two girls would be close in age. For the first time, the thought didn't hurt. Instead, it helped Kate to better understand what her own daughter might be interested in or doing with her time.

But what would it be like to be Joy? To have a loving, supportive husband at her side through the experience? To revel in the joy of the event, knowing the child would be welcomed and loved by both parents when it was born?

Jacob's gaze was on Kate and she forced herself to mask her emotions behind a pleasant smile. "Wh-what did you want to talk to me about?" she asked, wanting to change the course of her thoughts and the conversation.

"I want to invite you to our mothers-of-multiples group. We meet every other Thursday morning from nine to eleven at the church." Joy's pretty brown eyes were kind as she looked at Kate. "I would have told you sooner, but I didn't want to overwhelm you with too many details. Our next meeting is this Thursday. We have childcare for the children, giving the moms a chance to connect and offer each other support and encouragement. We also have a community specialist come in each time, and this week we have a CPR trainer coming."

Carter started to fuss, tired of being in the stroller, while just behind him, Bryce watched Joy quietly with his thumb in his mouth and behind him, Aiken still nibbled on his cracker.

What would she do if one of them choked? She'd never been trained in CPR—had never thought she might need it. But now, with three toddlers in her care, she'd be foolish not to learn.

Plus, it would give her the opportunity to spend more time with Joy.

"I'd love to come," she found herself saying. Even if she wasn't going to stay in Timber Falls to raise the boys, it wouldn't hurt to get a little support and encouragement while she was here.

On Friday morning, Jacob awoke with a light heart, though it took his foggy brain a minute to remember why he felt so happy.

That evening was the hayride and bonfire, and if the weatherman was correct, they'd have perfect weather for the event. The snow from earlier that week had already melted and they were enjoying a bit of unseasonal warmth.

Jacob whistled as he dressed, whistled as he drove Maggie to school and whistled as he walked into church.

"What has you so happy this morning?" his secretary, Bethiah Hubbard, asked when he walked into her office. She handed him a small stack of messages, which he took with a smile.

"It's a beautiful day, isn't it?" he asked.

She looked out the window, which faced the parking lot and Kate's house. "I suppose the sun is shining." A gleam of understanding suddenly lit her eyes. "Oh, I think I know what's going on."

Jacob rested his forearms on the high counter by her desk. "What's that?"

She shook her head, her short spiky hair, which was pink this week, wiggling on the top of her head as she grinned. "Mrs. Caruthers and Mrs. Topper stopped by yesterday to drop off the clean table linens and they told me you were taking Kate LeClair to the bonfire tonight."

"I'd be shocked if they hadn't told you." He laughed and then walked through the door that connected her office to his.

"I heard you've been to her house every night this week," Bethiah called after him.

"She's watching Maggie—I have to go there every night." He flipped on the switch to light up his office.

"But you've been eating supper there, too."

"The church ladies are bringing so much food it would be a shame to see it go to waste."

"Keep telling yourself that." Bethiah appeared at his door, her arms crossed and a teasing smirk on her face. "But I can see what's happening."

He pulled out the chair from behind his desk and met her raised-brow expression. "What?"

"You're falling for the actress."

"I am n—" He was about to deny the claim when he remembered his and Kate's agreement to pretend they were dating. He didn't have to lie to Bethiah, but he didn't have to divulge every detail. If he wanted the church ladies to believe the ruse, then he'd have to make everyone believe it.

"You're not going to deny my accusation?" she asked, the gleam still in her voice.

"My business is my business." He gave her a mock bow.

"Since when?" she asked with a laugh.

"Hello?" a lady called from Bethiah's office. "Anyone here?"

Bethiah gave Jacob a look that promised she wouldn't let this conversation end here, as she left the room to greet the visitor.

Jacob shook his head at Bethiah's insatiable need for gossip and looked at the stack of messages she'd handed to him. The first was from Mrs. Meacham, asking him to call her about the Christmas program.

Jacob sighed and leaned back in his chair, already exhausted. How could he forget? Mrs. Meacham was in charge of the Christmas program—not only was she in charge, she was the driving force behind it each year. With her broken hip, she wouldn't be able to oversee the program and they'd need to find someone else.

Maybe they could forego it this year—but that wouldn't work, either. Everyone would complain that it wasn't Christmas without the program.

A movement in Kate's yard drew Jacob's attention. She held one of the boys on her hip as she walked Carl Borland through the yard to the fence and pointed at the red spray paint. Carl owned the painting company. No doubt Kate had called him to repaint the fence—something Jacob had wanted to get to himself.

Kate was so beautiful, even from this distance, and Jacob allowed himself to watch her for a minute. He still couldn't believe how famous she was, but even though he'd felt a bit starstruck the first day after learning the truth, he rarely thought about it when he was with her. She was so humble and down-to-earth he had a hard time thinking about her being a star.

A thought came to him. Would Kate be interested in directing the Christmas program?

He immediately pushed the thought away and tried to wrack his brain to see who else was available. But the harder he tried to push Kate's name out of the possibilities, the more it tugged at him.

Would Kate even consider the idea? It seemed unlikely with all the work she had taking care of the boys—but if he asked, what was the worst she could say? No?

"Pastor?" Bethiah appeared at his door again. "One of your neighbors is here to see you."

Neighbor?

An older woman entered the office and Jacob immediately recognized her as Mrs. Graham who lived next to him in the house on the corner of Third Street and Broadway.

"Hello, Mrs. Graham. Please come in." He stood, happy to see the woman he'd been praying for since arriving in Timber Falls. She was in her midsixties, he'd guess, and every time he'd invited her to come to church, she had scoffed. So he'd stopped asking her. Instead, he and Maggie had tried to minister to her in other ways by mowing her lawn, shoveling her sidewalks and doing other odds jobs the widow could not do for herself.

"Now don't get all excited, thinking I've converted or anything." She pursed her lips and crossed her arms. "I just came because I have something I thought might interest you—or at least the woman taking care of those triplets."

"Kate?"

"Yeah, the actress. I've seen you at her house every day this week."

Bethiah coughed loudly in the next room.

"Would you like to have a seat?" he asked his neighbor, ignoring his secretary.

"This won't take long." She extended her hand

and set a thumb drive into Jacob's palm. "I have a security system, since I live alone, and one of my cameras caught the vandal who spray-painted that fence." She shook her head with disdain. "You might be surprised who it looks like."

Jacob frowned. "Who does it look like?"

"Rick Johnson's oldest son, Aaron."

"Aaron Johnson?" Jacob pulled back, stunned. "Are you sure?"

"No." She shrugged. "But it looks like a kid about his age and in the video you can see the front end of his brand-new silver Audi."

Sighing, Jacob shook his head. "I hope it's not Aaron."

"Well—" she lifted a sardonic eyebrow "—you shouldn't trust anyone—not even church kids."

It hurt to hear her say the words, but it hurt worse to know that somewhere along the way, someone had hurt her so deeply she didn't trust anyone.

"Thank you for bringing this to me." Jacob set it on his desk. "I'll look at it and see what we can do about the situation."

Mrs. Graham studied Jacob for a moment and then shook her head again. "Don't let that kid get away with this, just because his dad is a church elder. The worst thing you can do is turn a blind eye—I know because I speak from experience."

With that, she turned and left his office.

Chapter Eight

Kate didn't know why she felt so nervous as she stood in front of her bedroom mirror and looked over her appearance one more time. It was just a bonfire and hayride—with Jacob. What could be so nerve-racking about that? Hadn't she performed on stage, in front of thousands of people?

Maybe it was because during those performances, she'd been pretending to be someone else. If she was rejected, it was easier to believe her character was unlikable.

She felt far more vulnerable just being Kate.

"Kate?" Maggie's little voice echoed up the stairwell. "I'm here!"

If Maggie was here, then Jacob would be here, too.

Already, the church ladies had descended upon her home. They'd come a half hour early and spent their time playing with the boys and cleaning her house. They had instructed her to go upstairs and put on something nice.

"I'm in my room," Kate called out to Maggie.

A moment later, the little girl appeared at her bedroom door, out of breath from racing up the stairs. She stopped short, her eyes wide. "You look so pretty."

"Thank you." She hadn't wanted to over-dress—nor had she wanted to underdress. She hadn't been sure what to wear, so she had googled *what to wear to a hayride* and had taken Pinterest's suggestions. She wore a pair of dark blue jeggings, tall brown boots, and a chunky cream-colored cable-knit sweater with a cowl neck. She'd put soft curls in her hair and decided to wear it down. She'd bring a stocking cap if it got cold, but for now she left it off. The weather had been so nice the past few days.

"Daddy's waiting downstairs. He said the church ladies are going to make pizza with me tonight." Her eyes were huge with excitement. "Homemade!"

"That sounds yummy." Kate took a steadying breath and grabbed her purse. "I think I'm ready."

Maggie left Kate's door and raced down the steps and out of sight.

Slowly, Kate descended the stairs and found Jacob standing near the door, waiting for her.

Her breath caught at the sight of him and she couldn't stop her racing heart from skipping a beat.

Today, he looked nothing like a pastor. He wore a pair of tight blue jeans with a button-down shirt under his navy-blue peacoat. His chest was broad and his arms were muscular. For the first time since she'd met him, he wasn't clean-shaven. It lent a rustic quality to his appearance that she liked very much.

"Wow," he said, as he moved toward her. "You look great."

"So do you."

He smelled great, too.

Noise from the back of the house suggested everyone was busy in the kitchen.

"Are you ready to go?" he asked.

"I think so." She grabbed her jacket off the coat-tree and picked up her stocking cap and mittens. "Let me just say goodbye."

Walking toward the kitchen gave Kate a moment to collect herself. She had seen Jacob every day that week, so why was she reacting this way tonight?

All four church ladies were crammed into Kate's kitchen. The boys were in their high chairs, happily eating the chunks of pepperoni and cheese on their trays, and Maggie was already elbow-deep in pizza dough.

"Do you have everything you need?" Kate asked the group.

"We're right as rain," said Mrs. Topper with a grin, as she filled up one of the sippy cups.

"You go on and have a good time," Mrs. Anderson said from her spot at the stove, stirring sauce. "We have everything under control here."

"Okay." Kate kissed each of the boys and gave Maggie a side hug, and then said, "Good night."

"Good night," they all called back.

"Have fun," Mrs. Caruthers said with a smile.

Kate returned to the foyer where Jacob was waiting.

The sun was low in the clear sky when they walked out to his car. Though it was cool, it wasn't uncomfortable and Kate realized she probably wouldn't need her cap. The snow that had fallen earlier in the week had quickly melted, making it feel like fall again.

It took about twenty minutes to get to the farm and the whole way they enjoyed companionable conversation about the children and the church.

When they finally parked the car near one of the red outbuildings on the farm, nerves got the better of Kate again. What if Jacob's friends didn't like her? What if it was glaringly obvious that she didn't fit in? Everyone she had met at church seemed so wholesome and good. Would it be easy for them to spot all her flaws?

"Is everything okay?" Jacob asked, as he turned off the engine.

She marveled that he could read her so well. "I'll be fine."

"Are you sure? We can leave, if you'd rather not be here."

"It's not that." She tried to smile. "I'm actually really happy to be here."

"Good." The pleasure on his face was unmistakable. "So am I."

A large bonfire was already blazing in an open area beyond the barn, while a hay wagon waited for its passengers to board.

"Looks like they're getting the hayride going soon," Jacob said. "Shall we?"

They exited the car and walked across the barnyard toward the hay wagon. A beautiful white farmhouse sat off to the side and a collie ran from person to person, jumping happily. Hay bales, cornstalks and pumpkins dotted the house porch and decorated the yard.

At least two dozen people were either on the hay wagon or waiting to board. Kate recognized just a few of them from church, though she was certain many of the others must have been there, too.

"Jacob." A pretty woman in her later twenties called out to him from the line. "Come and join me."

Jacob hesitated and Kate looked up at his face to try to read his thoughts.

"Come on, Jacob!" she called again. "We're about to board."

"Do you mind joining Evelyn?" he asked Kate, his jaw a bit tense.

"Of course not." She'd pretty much go wherever Jacob wanted, if it meant she didn't have to face this crowd alone.

An older man sat at the front of the hay wagon in a pair of worn overalls, keeping the horses still, while another gentleman helped everyone step onto a hay bale and use it to get into the wagon bed.

"Oh, I'm so happy you've come," Evelyn said to Jacob when they reached her side. She put her hand on his arm and smiled up into his face, ignoring Kate. "You never come to the singles' events."

Thankfully, Jacob didn't ignore Kate like Evelyn had. "Evelyn, have you met Kate?" he asked.

Evelyn finally turned her large brown eyes to Kate, though they lacked the excitement she'd previously exhibited for Jacob. "I don't believe I've had the pleasure. Hello, Kate."

"Kate, this is Evelyn Ramsey." Jacob made

the introductions while the two women shook hands.

"I moved to Timber Falls about the same time as our Jacob." Evelyn put her perfectly manicured hand up to her lips. "Oops, I mean Pastor Jacob." She giggled. "We've become such good friends I forget to add the pastor part onto his name."

Kate just smiled.

Jacob didn't respond.

"I teach third grade at the Timber Falls Elementary School," Evelyn continued. "I keep telling Jacob if he'd get the church school built, I'd be his first applicant." She batted her eyelashes at Jacob. "Then he'd get to see me every day."

"We're working on it," Jacob said, looking beyond her, nodding hello at several other people who had noticed his arrival.

"I've heard the holdup has to do with Miss LeClair." Evelyn tilted her head and looked at Kate. "Don't you want to see progress in our little town, Miss LeClair?"

Sudden irritation made Kate's skin itch.

"It's not because of Kate," Jacob said quickly. "There are several factors in play."

Kate had thought quite a bit about the church's request to buy her home—Tabby's home. But she wasn't any closer to a decision. Once it was gone, it was gone. She'd only learned about Tabby's death one week ago—and was just feeling as if she was getting her feet under her. It was nice to have a little time away from the boys, just to clear her mind. Maybe tonight would be a good time to talk to Jacob about the house again.

"It's your turn to get on the wagon," Evelyn said to Kate.

Kate turned her attention to the wagon and suddenly realized how high it was. The hay bale they had put on the ground would not be sufficient enough to climb on board, and she hadn't been watching the others to see how they had done it.

"We're waiting patiently, Miss LeClair," Evelyn said with a sigh.

Kate wouldn't let Evelyn get to her—or stop her from having fun. She stepped onto the bale, shocked at how much it rocked, and reached for the wagon for support, but found Jacob's hand instead.

He took her hand in his and nodded at the wagon with an encouraging smile. "You'll have to climb on board. There isn't really a graceful way to do it."

She smiled, amazed again at how perceptive he was, and did as he instructed. She was just getting her footing in the hay when one of the horses spooked and jumped forward, causing Kate to fly into the middle of the wagon.

For a moment, she lay in the hay, facedown, stunned.

But in the next moment, a half dozen people were at her side.

"Are you okay?" Jacob asked, stepping onto the wagon and kneeling beside her.

The hay scratched her skin and stuck to her lips—and all she could think was that she wished she could burrow beneath it and disappear.

"I'm okay." She got onto her knees, removing the musty bits of hay from her mouth.

"It's in your hair, too." He gently reached up and started to remove the pieces.

The others had all stopped talking and were looking at her, their eyes wide.

Kate was mortified—but she had a choice. Either laugh it off—which she was certain many of them would join her in—or run from the scene in tears. Since she had more self-control than that, she decided to laugh.

And soon the others joined in.

"I suppose I'll never forget my first hayride," she said as she picked pieces of hay out of her sweater.

"That's one way to look at it." Jacob's eyes were shining with mirth as he offered his hand to her again and helped her stand. "Are you sure you're okay?"

"Nothing hurt but my pride."

"At least you weren't on a stage in front of thousands of people."

"A very small consolation."

The wagon was loaded to capacity and the only place that could possibly fit the two of them together was at the back of the wagon. "How does that look?" he asked.

"Perfect."

"Make room for me," Evelyn called to Jacob, as she climbed over someone to get to him.

"Sorry," Jacob responded. "There's barely enough space for the two of us." He took Kate's hand and led her to the back of the wagon.

They took a seat, their feet hanging over the edge, and were forced to sit very close to one another.

Kate tried to move, to give him a little more space, but there was nowhere to go.

Jacob looked down at their legs, which were pressed together, and then he looked up at her. His face was close to hers and she could see the darker specks of blue in his brilliant eyes. "Do you mind?" he asked softly.

She should mind—but she didn't—not in the least. She liked Jacob, far more than she should, and it scared her almost more than anything else in her life at the moment.

"It won't be hard for people to believe we're a couple," Kate said just as softly, thankful for the noise of the others as they talked all around them. "If we stay close, I mean."

"No." Jacob shook his head, his eyes caressing her face in the glow of the setting sun. "I have a feeling they're already talking. I know my secretary is."

"Do a lot of women throw themselves at you?" Kate glanced at Evelyn, who had shimmied between two men on the other side of the wagon and was talking incessantly. "As the pastor, I mean."

He glanced away from her, embarrassment in the set of his mouth. "More than you'd imagine. It doesn't really bother me, though, since I was warned by one of my mentors long ago that it would happen. It's Maggie that I get concerned about. She's not a fan of all the unwanted attention she gets from interested parties."

The horses went into motion with a jerk and Kate reached out on instinct for Jacob, putting her hand on his knee. He did the same, putting his arm around her shoulders to keep her on the wagon bed. But as the movement evened out, and she removed her hand from his knee, he kept his arm around her shoulders.

It was warm and comfortable, and she didn't mind at all.

She just hoped he didn't think she was yet one more woman throwing herself at him.

The scent of wood smoke lingered on their clothes and filled Jacob's car as he pulled up to the curb outside Kate's house at the end of the evening.

He and Kate sat in the car, the stars sparkling overhead, neither one anxious to get out.

Jacob turned off the engine and let the silence linger for a bit. "I had a lot of fun tonight, Kate. More fun than I've had in a long time. Thanks for being willing to sing at the campfire tonight."

"It was my pleasure."

Evelyn had made a big show of singling Kate out, asking her to sing. Kate had tried to refuse, but Evelyn was insistent. Jacob had been suspicious that Evelyn was trying to embarrass Kate, but like usual, Kate had been gracious. She had finally sung for everyone, her cheeks a bit pink, and had been humble as the crowd clapped and cheered for her at the end.

Evelyn had not looked happy at their praise and quickly turned the attention away from Kate.

"I had a lot of fun, too." She faced him and

he could just make out the form of her in the darkness. "Thank you for taking me. I've always wanted to go on a hayride, even if it did start out a little rocky."

"You're welcome." He grinned, thinking about how well she had handled the incident at the beginning of the evening when the horses had spooked and she'd ended up facedown in the hay. Her elegance and poise had shown through at that moment, too, and she had laughed off the embarrassment, allowing everyone else to laugh with her. It took a special kind of woman to put everyone at ease when she was probably mortified. He was quickly learning Kate LeClair was one-of-a-kind.

His smile dimmed and his heart suddenly started to race when he thought about the question he'd wanted to ask her all evening. "I've been wondering about Thanksgiving, which is less than a week away now." He fought the urge to rush through his question to just get it over with. Instead, he spoke gently and evenly, surprising himself with how calm he sounded. "I was wondering if you and the boys would like to join us for our Thanksgiving celebration."

She was silent for a moment. "You want to spend your holiday with us?"

Why did she sound so surprised?

"Isn't Thanksgiving for family?" she asked.

"Thanksgiving is for family *and friends.*" He wished they were still sitting close together on the wagon. "It's a time for people to give thanks for their many blessings—and that's exactly what you've become to Maggie and me. A blessing. We couldn't imagine celebrating any other way."

She looked down at her hands and he wished he could see her eyes better. They were so easy to read. Had he upset her?

"My parents will be coming from Iowa to spend the whole weekend with us." Jacob waited patiently for her to look back at him. "We'd love it if you could come, too."

"Your parents?"

"I'm their only child—and Maggie's their only grandchild. They come as often as they can."

She was quiet for a moment. "I'm honored that you would invite us." She paused. "But are you sure we wouldn't be an imposition? I'd hate to think you're inviting me out of pity or obligation."

Jacob almost laughed. Pity was the last thing he thought about where Kate was concerned. "There couldn't be anything further from my mind." *Or heart*, he wanted to add. "Maggie and I care very much for you and the boys. We want you to come—and I'd like you to meet my parents."

Again, she was quiet, and he was afraid he'd said too much.

"I'm not sure it's a good idea."

He frowned, wishing she would open up with him. What hurts did she hold inside? "Why not?"

Kate looked out the window toward her house and shook her head. It took her a moment to answer him. "I haven't had a normal Thanksgiving since I was eighteen—right before I ran away from home—and even then, it's wasn't a pleasant holiday."

She had never hinted at her past before, and he sensed that she didn't share it often. The knowledge that she'd trust him with part of it was an honor. "I'm sorry."

"It's not your fault." She turned back to look at him. "Jacob, you've been so kind to me this past week. I don't know where I would be right now without all you've done. But I don't belong here. You're all so good—"

"Kate, we're not as good as you think we are." His past mistakes returned to the fore-front of his mind with a vengeance. "All of us are sinners saved by God's grace. There is not one of us who are faultless. That's why Jesus came—not for the saint, but for the sinner." He was preaching to himself, just as much as he was to her. "Jesus doesn't expect perfection— and neither do I. I'd be a hypocrite if I did." He hoped he could speak to her heart. "If I required those who came to my home and my church to be faultless, I'd be alone. Worse, I wouldn't be welcome there, either. Maggie and I would love it if you and the boys would join us for Thanksgiving—not because you're perfect, but because you're you—and we like you exactly as you are."

She took a deep breath and let it out on a gentle exhale. "Well, if you put it that way." She laughed softly. "I'd love to come."

He couldn't stop the grin from spreading across his face. "Great. My parents will love to meet you."

"Please tell me what I can bring."

"Nothing—just those boys."

"I want to bring something."

He could tell it was important to her to contribute, so he nodded. "I'll ask my mom, who usually cooks the meal, and let you know."

"Thank you." She looked toward the house and reached for the door handle. "I should probably get inside."

"I've been meaning to ask you another question." He hadn't been brave enough to ask her about the Christmas program, in case she said no, but he was running out of time.

"Yes?"

"Mrs. Meacham has been in charge of the Christmas program at the church for as long as anyone remembers, but she's unable to do it this year." He swallowed the nerves in his throat. "I know you've only been to church once and you've got a lot going on, but I was wondering if you would—"

"Yes."

He stumbled to a stop. "Yes?"

"If you're wondering if I'll organize and lead the Christmas program, then the answer is yes—as long as you don't need a perfect person for that job, either."

Relief washed over him. "We'll take you as you are—but only if you're sure."

"Jacob, there's no possible way I could ever repay you or the church for everything you've done for me." She reached out and put her hand over his. "I'd be honored to give back this way."

Her hand was warm and soft on his and he had to fight the urge to capture it.

"We'll have volunteers to help watch the boys," he said, trying not to be distracted by her hand. "And I'm sure Mrs. Meacham could call you and let you know what she's done in the past—but you'd be free to do whatever you'd like."

She removed her hand from his. "I'll start working on it right away." She reached for the handle again. "But I should really get inside and relieve Mrs. Caruthers and the other ladies."

"Thank you," he said.

She smiled. "Would you like Maggie to spend the night? I have a feeling she's already asleep."

"Do you mind?"

Kate shook her head. "Never."

She started to open the door, but Jacob stopped her. "Let me," he said.

He jumped out of the driver's side and jogged around the back of the car to open her door.

"Thank you," she said softly, as she stood and faced him. "I'll call you in the morning to let you know when Maggie's ready to come home."

Without warning, she stood on her tiptoes and placed a kiss on Jacob's cheek.

"Good night," she whispered and then turned and walked to the house.

Jacob was speechless as he stood near the passenger door, his face on fire where she'd kissed him. The kiss had been so innocent, and so pure, that it had startled him.

Slowly, he closed the door and walked over to the driver's side where he got into the car and sat for a moment.

In just one week, Kate LeClair had slipped into his life as effortlessly as the shifting seasons—yet, he sensed that when she left, as he was certain she would, the transition would not be as smooth or as pleasant. That thought alone sobered his reaction to her kiss.

Chapter Nine

The first part of the week had gone by agonizingly slow—yet much too fast for Kate. It was already Wednesday and tomorrow she would be faced with meeting Jacob's parents. The thought made her stomach turn with nerves—*and* excitement.

Every day while the boys napped, Kate tackled another part of the house that needed to be sorted and organized. Though she had put hours of work into the effort, she felt like she hadn't even made a dent. There was literally a hundred years' worth of things to sort through, and she was afraid she was throwing or donating the wrong things. The boxes to donate to Goodwill had started to pile up on the front porch—but because of her uncertainty, the items that she felt she should keep for herself and the boys were still sitting where she'd found them. If she didn't keep the house, what would she do with everything? And would the boys really want the stuff she was saving?

The furniture was one of the harder things to consider. She didn't need it in her apartment in New York, yet she couldn't bear to sell it, either. Some of it looked handmade and she wondered if it had been made by one of her ancestors. It was priceless, really, and if she kept the house, she wouldn't move any of it.

But would she keep the house?

Her head hurt from going around and around the same questions without any answers.

On Wednesday afternoon, she sat in the living room with several plastic storage tubs filled with the clothes the triplets had already outgrown. At least here was something she could donate. They wouldn't need the clothes anymore and neither would Kate.

She pulled a tote toward her that said 0–3 months on the outside. She didn't need to go through all the clothing, but just wanted to make sure she wasn't accidentally donating something she shouldn't.

Taking off the lid, she wasn't prepared for the sight before her. The tiniest, sweetest clothing she'd ever seen laid within the container. Light blue, yellow, green and white outfits had been gently packed away by Tabby. Kate lifted one of the sleepers from the bin and held it, tears choking her throat. It was made of the softest material she'd ever touched and looked almost identical to the outfit that Kate had purchased for her own baby.

Memories flooded her heart unexpectedly, coming from the recesses where she'd put them to keep them out of the way. When Kate had been pregnant with her daughter, she had known almost immediately that she'd give the baby up for adoption. Every time she had passed a baby store, she had wanted to go inside but known it was pointless. There was no eager anticipation, no exciting preparations and no one to share the joy in the experience. She'd only given in to the urge once, to buy the little outfit, so she wouldn't send her baby into the world empty-handed.

Tabby, on the other hand, had probably spent hours preparing her heart and home for her boys. She had shopped, had a baby shower—a large one from the church, no doubt—and spent her pregnancy organizing the boys' room. Kate smiled at the thought.

Maybe Kate hadn't deserved to enjoy motherhood, but Tabby certainly had.

Yet, here Kate sat, in her cousin's home, with her cousin's babies asleep upstairs, and she was being given a second chance at motherhood. No, it wasn't how she had envisioned motherhood to look—especially because she was alone—but it didn't really matter. Maybe accepting her new role as a mother to the triplets was exactly what she needed to redeem the sins of her past. She couldn't parent her little girl, but she could parent the boys. It wouldn't be easy, but she could make it work—people with children made it work all the time. Yes, her life would look vastly different. But could she live with herself if she gave up three more children for adoption?

Giving up one had nearly destroyed her.

Kate hugged the little sleeper to her chest and inhaled a deep breath. The boys had no one else in the world. If Tabby wanted Kate to raise her babies, then who was Kate to say no? It was the greatest honor anyone could bestow upon her.

On the monitor, she heard one of the boys starting to fuss, so Kate laid down the sleeper and walked up the stairs to their bedroom.

Aiken stood in his crib, and when Kate entered the room, he offered her a slobbery grin. "Mamamama," he said, while he held the crib railing and jumped with glee.

His excitement at seeing her brought more tears to her eyes. In a very short time, she had become the center of their little universe. They'd already lost one mama. She couldn't be the reason for them to lose another.

The knowledge that she'd made at least one decision—the most important one—made her heart lighter than it had been in a long time. She walked across the room and lifted Aiken out of his crib, holding him close. The other two continued to sleep, so she tiptoed out of the room and gently closed the door again.

A knock at the front door brought her back downstairs. "Who could that be?" she asked Aiken.

He found her necklace and started to play with it, unconcerned about their visitor.

When they arrived downstairs, they found a middle-aged woman standing on the front porch with a smile plastered to her face.

Kate opened the door. "May I help you?"

"I'm Mrs. Johnson," she said. "I'm scheduled to bring your supper today." She walked into the foyer without being invited and continued to talk. "I know I'm much too early, but I have other commitments this evening. You see, my son Aaron is an honor student and he's being inducted into the National Honor Society at the high school tonight."

Kate closed the door. "How ni—"

"I made lasagna, though I haven't baked it yet. You do think you could manage to bake the lasagna, don't you?"

"Yes, of cour—"

"And I've also brought garlic bread, a salad that will need to be dressed and a vegetable medley that should be baked, as well." She started to walk toward the kitchen. "I've written instructions for everything."

"It's so kind of you—"

"I'm assuming the kitchen is back here." She paused to wait for Kate's response, but Kate was almost too afraid to give one. Instead, she nodded.

The lady continued toward the kitchen. "I've heard that you've met my husband, Rick."

"At church two Sundays ago."

"He is very concerned for you." Mrs. Johnson set her bags on the table in the kitchen, which Kate had managed to keep clean that day.

"Concerned?" Kate asked.

"Yes. We heard about the vandalism on your property—everyone has—and we just want to make sure you're safe."

"I feel very safe." Kate bounced Aiken who'd started to fuss for his sippy cup, which was still on his high chair from lunchtime.

"Well, you're a stronger woman than I am." Mrs. Johnson pulled several containers from her bag and opened the refrigerator to put them inside. "This neighborhood is not what it used to be. I wouldn't want to raise my children here."

"This neighborhood?" Kate glanced out the

windows and saw the back of the library. She also had a view of the playground, which was full of little children and their parents.

"The vandalism is just the beginning," Mrs. Johnson said, as she finished putting the containers of food away. "Next, it will be robberies and possibly assaults." She leaned forward, as if she were talking to a confidante. "If you ask me, I think it's because of the library."

Kate blinked several times. "The library?"

"People coming and going all day, you know."

"Um—"

"Well, who am I to gossip?" Mrs. Johnson sighed and folded her fabric bags until she had a neat little pile. "If you're accosted in your sleep, don't say I didn't warn you. Now, I must be off."

Kate could do nothing but stare as the woman left her kitchen.

"Goodbye," Mrs. Johnson called.

Pulling her senses together, Kate rushed into the foyer. "Thank you for supper."

"It's no trouble." She waved her hand and then stepped outside.

Silence fell over the house as Aiken and Kate stared after the woman. Kate had no idea what to make of Mrs. Johnson or her strange musings.

Kate's phone rang in the living room, so she set Aiken in his toy room and then grabbed her phone.

It was Jacob.

A smile warmed her face. The only day that week that she hadn't spent time with him was Saturday, the day after the hayride. After breakfast, Maggie had run across the street and then she and her dad had spent the day together.

His words, which had been such a balm to her soul the night of the hayride, had returned to her many times that week. Was it possible that she could be accepted by this community, even though she wasn't perfect?

The phone continued to buzz, so she pressed the green icon. "Hello."

"Hi," he said in a familiar, friendly tone. "How are you?"

Aiken played quietly in the next room, so Kate took a seat on the couch and looked at the bins of clothes stacked near the door. "I'm good. Really good." Should she tell him she'd finally decided to keep the boys?

"You sound good. I happened to see Mrs. Johnson leave your house. No doubt she brought you her famous lasagna."

Mrs. Johnson's strange visit returned to her mind. "She did—and she had some interesting things to say."

"Uh-oh. That doesn't sound good."

"She heard about the vandalism and told me how dangerous this neighborhood has become."

Kate leaned back against the couch. "If I didn't know better, I'd think she was trying to scare me off."

"She probably was." He sighed. "I have a meeting with her husband in about twenty minutes and I'm not looking forward to it."

"I'm sorry."

"It's fine. But I'd rather hear what made you so happy."

She paused for a moment and then plunged forward. "I made a decision today."

"A good one?"

"I've decided to keep the boys."

"Kate, that's wonderful. I'm so glad. I've been praying you would have clarity about the matter."

Her heart warmed at the knowledge that his prayers were covering her. That he cared enough about her to bother. "If I'm honest with myself, from the moment I heard about Tabby and Adam, there wasn't any other option in my mind. I just needed some time to process. They're my only family and we need each other." Her only family, besides her daughter, though she'd probably never see her again.

"I know the boys don't understand, but if they did, I'm sure they'd be celebrating right now."

She smiled, her world expanding in ways

she'd never thought possible now that she knew she'd be a mom—forever.

Tears suddenly filled her eyes. She was a mom.

"Hey, Kate?"

She swallowed the tears. "Yes?"

"Are you okay?"

"Just a little emotional at the moment." She tried to laugh, but it came out like a sob.

"Do you want me to come over? I am literally sitting in my office right now, looking at your house. I could be there in a second."

Kate wiped away her tears and stood to look out the window at the church. "No, I'm fine—and you have a meeting soon." She moved aside the curtain and saw him sitting at his desk. She waved at him and he waved back. "Why did you call? It certainly wasn't to hear me cry."

He laughed. "I called to let you know my parents will be in town by noon tomorrow and my mom said she'd love for you to come over right away. She said if you'd like, she could use some help getting the Thanksgiving supper ready."

Tomorrow. Thanksgiving. Jacob's mom. The nerves returned like a tidal wave.

"I told her you were a guest," Jacob said quickly, "and we shouldn't put you to work, so if you'd rather not—"

"I would like to help your mom." She could

still see him at his desk, though he was too far away to make out his facial features.

"Good." She could tell by the sound of his voice that he was smiling. "She'd like that, too."

"I just wish she'd let me bring something."

"She knows how hard it is for you to get to the store with the boys, so she's bringing all the groceries."

"That's very thoughtful of her."

"I think you'll like my mom." His voice was smiling again. "I've always been crazy about her."

Kate's heart warmed at his words and she found she liked Mrs. Dawson already.

"I should go," Kate said. "It sounds like Carter and Bryce are awake."

She waved at him from her window and he waved back.

"I'll be by to pick up Mags after work," he said.

"If you'd like to plan on staying for supper, Mrs. Johnson brought way more than the boys and I can ever eat."

"I'd like that. Goodbye, Kate."

"Bye, Jacob."

Jacob hung up the phone and set it on his desk, a smile on his face.

"Will you be joining her for supper tonight,

too?" Bethiah asked from the outer office, peeking around the corner of the door to raise her eyebrow at him. "I'm just wondering what I can feed to the gossip mill."

He grabbed a piece of paper and wadded it into a ball and then threw it across his office, through the door and hit her on the shoulder.

Bethiah laughed and shook her head.

"If you two are done." Rick Johnson stood at Jacob's door, an impatient frown on his face. "Could we have our meeting?"

Rick's presence was like a splash of cold water. Jacob instantly sobered and stood to shake the head elder's hand. "I wasn't expecting you for another fifteen minutes."

"I can see that." Rick walked into Jacob's office and took a seat near the desk.

Jacob closed the door connecting his office to Bethiah's, and then he turned back to Rick. "Could I get you something to drink?"

"I'm not staying long. What is it you want to discuss?"

Jacob tried to draw from all his uncomfortable experiences as a pastor in the past. This wasn't the first time he'd had to confront someone from his congregation and it probably wouldn't be the last. He just knew it might be the hardest.

Sitting at his desk, Jacob opened his laptop

and waited for the screen to turn on. "Did you hear about the vandalism at Kate's house last week?"

"I saw it with my own eyes."

"A neighbor across the street was able to catch the vandal on tape." Jacob turned his computer to face Rick. "It's hard to tell from this distance, but it looks like a teenage boy and you can see that the front of his car looks just like Aaron—"

"Are you suggesting my son vandalized Miss LeClair's home?" He looked at Jacob with anger and disbelief in his eyes. "How dare you accuse him."

"I'm not accusing him—I'm just showing you the footage, and pointing out that the car the vandal used looks just like a silver Audi."

"Aaron's Audi is not the only one in town."

"Yes, but there aren't many."

"This proves nothing." He leaned back in the chair and put one ankle over his knee. "Why did you call me away from my law firm to show this to me?"

"For several reasons. The first is that the vandal resembles your son, and the second is that Miss LeClair is our neighbor and a prospective member of the church. As an elder, I thought you should be aware of the situation."

"The *head* elder," he corrected.

"All the more reason to bring it to your attention."

Rick stared at Jacob. "Is that all?"

Jacob sighed. "For now, until I have more proof."

"As the *head* elder, and one of your bosses," Rick leaned forward, "I'd suggest you step lightly where my son is concerned."

"Is that a threat?" Jacob detested bullies.

"No. Just a friendly reminder." He ran his hand along his comb-over. "And here's another one. You're running out of time regarding the school." He pointed at Kate's house. "I want her consent to sell by Christmas—no later. Do you understand?"

"I'm not in control of Miss LeClair's decision." Anger boiled just beneath the surface of Jacob's calm demeanor, though he refused to give in to it. "I will not pressure her when she has so many other things to consider."

"If you won't pressure her, then maybe it's time we found someone else to do your job."

It was another threat and Jacob wouldn't bite the bait.

"I think our meeting is over." Jacob stood and extended his hand. "If you'll excuse me, I have other pressing matters."

Rick Johnson also stood, but he just scowled at Jacob's hand and then strode out of the office.

A second later, Bethiah opened the door and poked her head around the corner. "That was intense."

"I closed the door for privacy."

"Which I gave you, while I listened from the other side." She grinned. "He's a bully. Don't let him get to you."

"My thoughts exactly." Though, as the head elder, Rick had power over Jacob's job.

"Good. Now, I'm making a fresh pot of coffee. Would you like some?"

"Yes." He took his seat again. "And make it extra strong. I'm going to need it."

"You got it." Bethiah started to sing as she left their office, her off-pitch voice full of joy.

Not for the first time, Jacob thanked God for providing him with a secretary who had a sense of humor. As a pastor, he needed it more often than he liked.

Chapter Ten

At exactly noon, Kate pushed the stroller across the street to Jacob's house. She had never been inside before, and though she was excited to see what it looked like, she was far more anxious to meet Jacob's parents. Would they like her? Would they wonder why Jacob had invited her?

"Kate!" Maggie opened the front door even before Kate pushed the stroller off the street and onto the sidewalk. The air was brisk and the sky was overcast. Snow was forecasted again, but this time they were expecting quite a storm. Thankfully, she didn't have far to go to get home, or she might have needed to cancel.

An older woman appeared behind Maggie in the doorway. She wore her light brown hair in a pixie style, sweeping across her forehead. She was tall and trim and wore blue jeans with a beautiful mauve sweater and scarf around her neck. She was what Kate would consider a timeless beauty—but it was her eyes and the laugh lines around her mouth that made Kate take to her immediately.

They reminded her of Jacob.

"Look at those boys!" Mrs. Dawson said, as she stepped out onto the porch with her hands on Maggie's shoulders. "I've heard so much about them. Mags can't stop talking about you or the babies."

Kate tried not to be self-conscious as she walked up the sidewalk. "Hello, Mrs. Dawson."

Mrs. Dawson extended her hand, which was also long and slender. "Just call me Mary."

The boys squealed at seeing Maggie and she jumped and clapped at their excitement.

"I can see their affection for one another is mutual," Mary said with a laugh.

"They adore her—and so do I." Kate gave Maggie a quick hug.

"Let's get them inside," Mary suggested with a warm smile, "and then you and I can be properly introduced. Jake already has the turkey in the oven, so you and I can chat for a while before we start cooking."

Jake? Kate had never heard anyone call him that.

"Grammy said I could help cook, too," Maggie said.

Jacob came to the door, slipping his coat on as he walked toward them. "Hello, Kate."

She glanced up and her heart skipped a beat at the sight of him. "Hello."

"Do you need help with the boys?" he asked.

She nodded, thankful for a distraction from her traitorous nerves.

One by one, Kate took the boys out of the stroller and handed Carter and Bryce to Jacob and Mary. She took Aiken and followed them into the parsonage, leaving the stroller on the front porch.

Kate paused just over the threshold, stunned at the interior. "This is breathtaking," she said in awe. "I feel like I've walked into a museum."

Jacob glanced around his home. "Don't let the furniture stop you from feeling comfortable."

"On the contrary." She shook her head. "It kind of makes me feel like I'm in a fairy tale."

Mary smiled at Jacob, as only a mother could, and then she looked back at Kate. "I have some tea ready for us. Would you like to join me?"

"I would love to."

"Good. I'll just take this little guy and get everything set up while you hang up your coat." She left the foyer with Carter in her arms and went into the dining room.

"Here." Jacob used one arm to hold Bryce and

the other to help Kate with her coat. "Mags, can you hang up Kate's coat, please?"

"Sure!"

"Thank you," Kate said to the little girl.

Jacob didn't hide his admiration as he looked Kate over. She had chosen to wear a simple dark green maxi dress with long sleeves and a brown belt. She also wore a long necklace and her hair was swept up into a loose bun.

"You look lovely," he said.

Her cheeks grew warm. "Thank you."

He looked great, too. But before she could compliment him, he poked his head into the front parlor and then said, "My dad's around here somewhere." He shrugged. "People tend to get lost in this rambling old house pretty easily—consider yourself warned."

Kate laughed at the thought.

"I'm here, I'm here." A tall man pushed through a swinging door in the dining room. He looked a lot like Jacob, only thirty years older and with graying hair. "I wouldn't get myself lost when I knew this lovely young woman was coming over—I was just snitching from the kitchen."

Mr. Dawson's face was just as kind and welcoming as his wife and son. He extended his large hand to Kate. "And before you go and make me feel old by calling me Mr. Dawson, the name is Jim."

Kate took his hand, surprised at the strength in it. "It's nice to meet you, Jim."

"Jake told us you're a stage actress." Jim stood next to his son, but he addressed Kate.

"Yes, I am."

"I've done some community theater myself." He grinned. "I even played Cyrano de Bergerac once and received a standing ovation from a theater of *five hundred* people."

Jacob shook his head. "Dad—"

"That's wonderful," Kate said quickly, not wanting Jacob to tamper his dad's excitement.

Jim crossed his arms and leaned forward. "I volunteer for our theater company in Ames, Iowa, but I've always wondered if there's money to be made. Do you make a decent living?"

"Dad," Jacob tried again.

"It's okay," Kate said with a smile. She knew Jim wasn't being nosy, but genuinely curious. "I do make a decent living—but it wasn't always that way. It took me several years to land a role that paid well. At different times in my life, I've worked two or three jobs just to support my acting."

"You don't say?" Jim shook his head. "But you've got a steady role now?"

"Dad—"

"I do."

"Anything I might know?"

"Dad," Jacob said with a sigh. "I told you Kate is part of the Broadway tour of *Les Misérables*."

Jim turned back to Kate, surprise on his face. "You don't say? Broadway?"

"I told you," Jacob said, shaking his head. "On the phone."

"You must have told your mom."

"I told both of you." Jacob laughed. "Last Saturday when I called—you and mom both picked up an extension."

"I remember you calling, and I remember you telling us Kate is a stage actress, but I'd definitely recall if you mentioned she was on Broadway."

Jacob gave an exasperated sigh and Kate couldn't help but laugh.

"I think my son's memory is worse than mine." Jim put his arm around Kate's shoulders and led her to the dining room where Mary was still holding Carter, putting the finishing touches on the tea. The table was set with beautiful pink china on a fine lace tablecloth. It held several platters of cookies, scones, muffins and fruit. Two different pots of tea were steaming on their trivets, and cubes of sugar sparkled from a bowl.

Kate's eyes grew wide at the spread. "This looks amazing."

"Since we're eating supper a bit late," Mary said with a smile, "I thought we should have a little something to tide us over."

"Why don't you have a seat?" Jim held a chair out for Kate and leaned over to whisper, "Mary's blueberry tea and sugar cookies are my favorite."

Kate smiled at him and he winked.

"I had no idea you'd go to such trouble," Kate said to Mary.

She waved aside Kate's comment. "There's nothing better than a cup of tea to get to know one another."

Jacob followed them into the dining room with Bryce in his arms and Maggie right behind him. "Don't overwhelm her with too many questions about Broadway." He sent a pointed look at his father and then glanced at Kate. "He probably enjoys musical theater even more than you do."

"Your mom is a close second," Jim said to Jacob, as he went around the table and held the chair out for Mary and then pulled Maggie onto his lap, taking a seat next to his wife.

Jacob sat on the chair next to Kate, a smile on his face. "Don't let them fool you. They saw you play Fantine when you were in Chicago.

They're avid fans of yours." He leaned close to her and said quietly—but loud enough for them to hear, "They're just trying to be cool."

His parents protested his remark, making Kate laugh. "So you knew all along?" she ask his dad.

Jim put up his hands. "Guilty as charged."

"Jake is right," Mary said. "We did see you in Chicago and thought you were magnificent, though we had no idea who you were until Saturday when Jake told us."

"But don't worry." Jim wrapped his arms around Maggie who grinned. "We won't pester you about it too much. To us, you're simply Jake's good friend and neighbor, and we're so happy he invited you to join us."

Kate glanced at Jacob and found him offering a cookie to Bryce. He met her gaze and the fond look in his eyes warmed her heart.

It felt nice to have a good friend.

"I notice you call him Jake," she said, changing the subject. "No one else calls him that."

"We named him after my father," Jim said. "Reverend Jacob Alexander Dawson. To differentiate the two, we called this one here Jake."

"Do you prefer Jake?" she asked Jacob.

"He once told me that he let us call him Jake," Mary lifted one of the teapots and poured the hot liquid into her cup. "Because he loved us.

The only other person who called him Jake was his wife, Laura."

Jacob sat quietly, his expression a mixture of emotions.

"So, if he ever tells you to call him Jake—" Jim handed a cookie to Maggie and then smiled at Kate "—consider yourself one of his favorite people."

Kate didn't think she'd ever have that honor, but tucked it away in her heart, nonetheless.

"Shall we change the subject?" Jacob asked.

"Are we making you uncomfortable?" Mary asked her son with a playful bat of her eyes.

"Just a bit."

"Then let's find something else to talk about." She looked at her husband. "Did you bring Jake's baby book?"

"It's somewhere—"

"Remind me not to invite them next time," Jacob said to Kate. "I can't take them anywhere."

The laughter filled the room and Kate joined in, noticing how the boys sat contentedly on the adults' laps, taking in everything around them.

And suddenly, Kate wanted to offer them a home and family just like this—yet, she knew their lives would look very different being raised by a full-time actress in the city. Was she doing the right thing by them?

Doubts started to invade her happy mood and it took everything in her willpower to rejoin the conversation and be fully present with the people around her, knowing it couldn't always be this way.

Laughter trickled out from the kitchen as Jacob sat with his dad in the back parlor and played a game of chess. The boys were taking their afternoon nap upstairs and his mom, Kate and Maggie were busy with supper preparations.

Outside, the world had quickly turned into a winter wonderland with snow falling thick from the sky. It already gathered on tree limbs and buildings, coating everything in a fresh new blanket.

"I have a feeling you'd rather be in the kitchen than here with me," Dad said, as he moved his rook and took one of Jacob's pawns.

Jacob shook his head and examined the board. "What makes you think that?"

"I haven't beaten you in chess since you were eleven."

"That's not true."

"Almost." His dad leaned back in his chair. "And every time a peal of laughter comes out of that room, you look like you're missing out on the most important event of the year."

It was no use denying his dad's claims. Ever since he was a kid, his dad had been able to see right through Jacob. "It sounds like they're having a great time."

"You like her, don't you?" Dad asked.

Jacob didn't lift his eyes from the board. "I've only known her for two weeks."

"It doesn't matter." His dad shrugged. "When you know, you know. I knew it the first night I met your mom."

"I remember the story." He'd heard it a hundred times, at least. His parents had met at a dance, though his mom had come with a different date. By the end of the evening, the date was so tired of his mom dancing with his dad, the date had left without telling her, and his dad had walked her home. They were engaged a month after the night they'd met and were married two weeks after that.

Neither one had regretted it for a single day.

"You knew the first time you met Laura, didn't you?" his dad asked cautiously. "Is that what's holding you back? Laura?"

It was no use. Jacob couldn't concentrate on the chess game now. He leaned back in his chair and faced his father. "I did know the first time I met Laura—but life was a lot less complicated then."

"You didn't answer my original question. Do you like Kate?"

Jacob folded his hands across his chest. "To be honest, I haven't even allowed myself to contemplate that question."

"Why not?"

"Because we live in two very different worlds." And the truth was he had no wish to acknowledge his feelings when he knew Kate would probably be gone in less than a month.

"She lives across the street—you couldn't be any closer."

"You know what I mean. She has a job that requires her to live in New York and travel the country. I have a job that literally requires me to walk across the street."

"Fiddlesticks." His dad waved aside Jacob's response. "I see how she looks at you and how much she enjoys being here today. She's longing for a home and a family." He smiled. "She has a family—now she just needs a home and a husband."

"Dad." Jacob shook his head. "It's ridiculous to even discuss this. She's not interested in me."

"How do you know? Have you asked her?"

He frowned. "Of course not."

"Then how do you know?"

How did he know? "I just do."

"Does she call you?"

He shrugged. "On occasion."

"Does she invite you over?"

Jacob had been at her house almost every day for two weeks. "Yes."

"Does she go out of her way to do things for you, to compliment you, to show you how much she appreciates you?"

Jacob rubbed his face in frustration. "None of that means she's interested. Besides, I don't even know if I want her interested." His voice lowered a notch as the past reared its ugly head. "I loved Laura with all my heart. We had an amazing relationship and I feel blessed beyond measure. Who am I to ask God for another love story? I'm the last person to deserve it."

His dad frowned. "I've never heard so much rubbish in my life."

"What?"

"Jake." His father leaned forward and put his elbows on his knees. "Our heavenly Father is in the business of blessings. It is His desire to give His children extravagant blessings—why would you put a limit on Him?"

"Because I don't deserve it." Emotions clogged Jacob's throat and he had to pause to gather himself. "I messed up with Laura. Why would God give me a second chance?"

"Do you honestly think Laura's death was your fault?" His dad pulled back and frowned.

Jacob couldn't meet his gaze. "Part of it, yes."

"I'm surprised at you, Jake."

Even though he was a grown man, his father's rebuke still stung.

"God is sovereign," his dad said. "No matter what we do, if we desire to serve Him with all our hearts, and do not willfully disobey, His will will be done."

"But if I hadn't pushed Laura to get pregnant with Maggie—"

"If God couldn't fix our messes, where would any of us be? Look at Abraham and Hagar, David and Bathsheba—even Peter. They all messed up, yet God was sovereign." Dad reached across the low table and put his hand on Jacob's knee. "I don't know why God allowed Laura to die, but I do know that He's not done with your story. Don't put God in a box or limit His blessings in your life. He wants to give you good things—and that might mean another wife. Don't deny the possibilities."

Jacob put his hand on his dad's and nodded. "Where are you when I'm counseling my parishioners?"

Dad smiled and patted Jacob's knee. "I think you do a mighty fine job, son."

His dad's praise was the highest approval Jacob valued and he let it sink in and fill his doubting heart.

"Now." His dad put his hand on his chin and squinted at the chessboard. "How many moves do you think I have left before I win?"

Jacob smiled and shook his head. It was time to get his head back in the game.

Chapter Eleven

"That was great," Kate said to the little boy who had just auditioned for the part of a Wise Man in the Christmas program. "I'll post the cast list on the church website by the end of tomorrow." She handed the little boy's mom a flyer with information about rehearsal times. "Everyone will get a part," she said to both the mom and child. "Thank you for auditioning, I know it's not how you've usually done—"

"We're so honored you have agreed to direct the program this year," the mom said. "It's not every day that Broadway is brought to Timber Falls."

Kate smiled and accepted the compliment as if it were the first, and not the hundredth, that day. "We'll see you next week for rehearsal, Jetson," she said to the little boy.

"Bye!" He waved to her as he raced out of the sanctuary, his mom trailing behind.

"I think that's it." Jacob walked into the sanctuary and nodded at the mom as they crossed paths.

"Whew." Kate leaned back in the front pew where she'd been watching auditions. Jacob had brought her a table and it was now strewn with papers. "I lost count. How many kids did you see running around here this afternoon?"

"At least a hundred."

"And I have to find *all* of them parts in this program?"

Jacob sat on the pew and shrugged. "Mrs. Meacham gave the main parts to the best actors, threw in several manger animals and made the rest a choir of angels."

A few children had stood out to her that day, and she had a good idea which ones would play Mary, Joseph, the Shepherd and the Wise Men. She also knew that Maggie would play the lead angel, with her sweet disposition and clear voice.

"If you need any help remembering who is who, just let me know," Jacob said. "I know a lot of them—though, there were several who came that don't go to church here. They must have heard you're directing the program and wanted to be a part of something great. I think the most Mrs. Meacham ever had in the program is fifty-five."

"You flatter me."

He shrugged. "Just speaking the truth."

Kate gathered her papers and then stood. Her back was stiff from sitting on the hard pew for the past few hours. They had decided to hold the auditions on the Monday evening after Thanksgiving, so it had grown late and her stomach rumbled with hunger.

"Mrs. Caruthers and Mrs. Anderson brought the boys and Maggie to your house about an hour ago to feed them." Jacob also stood. "I hope that's okay. I didn't want to interrupt you to ask, since you had quite the line of actors waiting to audition."

"That's fine. I'm thankful they were willing to do that."

He watched her as she straightened the stack of papers and put them into a folder. "They also made another offer." He crossed his arms and didn't quite meet her gaze.

"What kind of offer?"

"They offered to stay with the kids if you and I wanted to go out and get something to eat."

Kate paused. The matchmakers had quieted down and weren't bothering Kate and Jacob like they had been at first. Not only did Jacob and Kate make a point to be seen together on Sunday mornings, Jacob had also invited Kate to the Ashers' Christmas fundraiser, which would be held in two weeks—but it appeared that the church ladies hadn't fully stopped their match-making ways and wanted to see more. "And what did you say?"

"I, uh, said yes—just to keep up the ruse that we're a couple."

The ruse. She nodded. *Of course.*

Ever since Thanksgiving Day, Kate had tried hard not to think about how much she had come to care for Jacob. He had shown her no reason to hope that he had feelings for her, and even if he had, she was growing more and more convinced that she needed to start making plans to return to the tour. She had three babies to care for now, and other than the theater, she had no real skills or abilities to provide for them. It would be foolish to give up a steady-paying job—especially when she had no guarantee of a future in Timber Falls.

"Do you mind?" he asked with a frown. "We can always say no."

"I don't mind." She shook her head. "I just don't want to be an imposition."

"They offered—and more than that, they love being with the children." He indicated the door. "Are you ready to go?"

She grabbed her coat and slipped it on, and

then followed him out of the sanctuary with her folder in hand.

Jacob flipped several switches, turning off all the lights, leaving them in darkness.

Kate waited by the back door, her breath loud in her ears, as the stillness of the empty church echoed around her.

"Do you enjoy being a pastor?" she asked when he finally joined her at the door.

He pushed the door open to reveal a world of white sparkling snow. Tonight, the moon was high and bright, casting shadows over the earth.

"I do—on most days." He smiled and closed the door behind her. After locking it, he shook the handle once to make sure it was secure and then he led her to his car.

The air was cold and Kate shivered, so she was thankful his car was warm.

"Remote start," he said when he got into the driver's seat. "I started it from my office a couple minutes before I came to get you." He put the key in the ignition and then shifted it into Drive. "And to elaborate on my answer, I do love my job—but it's more than a job. It's a lifestyle. My work is so intertwined with my daily life I couldn't imagine one without the other. This church—" he motioned to the large imposing structure as they passed on the street "—is an extension of my home."

"I like that."

"They say it takes a village to raise a child—and the church is very much my village. I couldn't imagine raising Maggie any other way, especially without a mom. The church ladies, for all their meddling ways—" he smiled "—are godly women who are living by example. They adore Maggie and she adores them. I thank God for them every day."

Kate considered her own lifestyle and how it would look as she raised the boys. Her cast was her family, and she knew they would welcome the boys on tour in a heartbeat—but were they the kind of role models she wanted the boys to have? Of course, they were wonderful, loving people, but very few of them were people of faith, and even though that hadn't been part of Kate's life in the past—after living in Timber Falls, she couldn't imagine it not being a part of her life going forward. For at least a year longer, she would have no steady church family—and when she returned to New York, she didn't even know where to begin looking for a church like the one in Timber Falls.

"You're a little reflective tonight." Jacob turned the car onto Main Street and parked it in front of Ruby's Bistro. Already, the downtown had turned into a charming Christmas village. Garland, ribbons, bells and lights adorned the street from beginning to end. Window displays had toys, Christmas trees and manger scenes. "Is everything okay?"

"Just thinking about the future," she said.

Jacob put the car in Park but didn't turn off the engine. He faced her, his voice a bit hesitant. "Have you decided what you want to do with the house?"

Her phone dinged and the screen lit up in her purse. She could only see the top but it was another Facebook notification. Kate had finally updated her page to let her fans know she was well and taking a leave to deal with family issues.

What ensued were thousands of comments from well-wishers, offering prayers and good thoughts. Many held tickets for upcoming shows on the tour and told her they hoped she'd be back in time for them to see her. Still others, who had gone to performances since she left, were bummed—and some even angry—that she hadn't been on stage.

"There are still thirteen months left in my contract," she said to Jacob gently. "Which my agent has been reminding me about daily. It would be foolish for me to drop out now—especially when I've worked so hard to get here."

Jacob faced the steering wheel again but didn't speak.

More than anything, Kate wanted him to protest what she had just said—to give her even the smallest sign that he cared about her and didn't want her to leave.

Yet, even as she longed for him to tell her to stay, she knew it was an impossible idea. He had tried to convince her that no one in his church was faultless, and she agreed with him—but it was one thing to be an imperfect parishioner, another to be the spotless wife of a pastor. Jacob needed someone like his first wife, Laura, to lead by example. From all accounts, Laura had been an amazing woman. Brilliant, beautiful and compassionate. She was a healer, a woman who longed to go into medicine because God had called her to minister to His people right alongside her husband.

Kate could never be like Laura. It was too late for that. What would the church think if they knew the pastor's wife had given up a baby for adoption when she was a teenager? Right now, the church looked up to Jacob and respected him. Her reputation would only hurt his and she could never live with herself.

It was better if he didn't try to convince her to stay—which, thankfully, he wasn't.

"What about the boys?" he asked, interrupting her thoughts.

"I've already spoken to my producer. She said

she will start to look for a nanny who would be willing to travel with us. The children on cast have tutors who go from city to city with them. It wouldn't be unheard of for me to take along a nanny."

"And the house?" he asked quietly.

"I'm still not sure. Part of me wants to keep it and possibly rent it out—just so that I can have it for the boys when they get older." She shrugged. "Or when I retire from acting and need a place to live."

"When might that be?" he asked quietly.

"Not for several years. I'll work on stage as long as possible."

Jacob set his hands on the steering wheel but still didn't look at her. "When will you rejoin your show?"

"I still have a lot to do at the house and my agent said I should take the entire six-week leave, no matter how much my producer is pushing me to come back early."

He finally looked at her, his emotions masked behind his eyes. "So we still have you until Christmas?"

We still have you.

His words meant more than he could possibly realize.

It had been a long time since she'd felt like she belonged somewhere.

"The tour comes to Minneapolis on December twenty-third," she said. "Which means I will have to leave before Christmas."

"Do you have a show on Christmas day?"

She shook her head.

"Minneapolis is only two hours away." He studied her in the shadows of the car. "Do you think it would be possible for you and the boys to come back and spend the day with Maggie and me? A sort of farewell?"

Kate hated goodbyes—especially ones she didn't want to say. But how could she say no to him when she didn't want to? She opened her mouth to start answering, but he interrupted her.

"My parents plan to come back and Laura's parents will also make the trip from Ohio. I know they'd all love to have you join us."

Laura's parents?

Kate swallowed the disappointment she felt. How could she possibly meet Laura's parents? She'd feel like an intruder. No doubt they'd wonder why their son-in-law had invited a single woman to join them—and she wouldn't want them to jump to conclusions that might hurt them.

"I don't think it will work," she said, looking toward Ruby's Bistro so he couldn't see the regret on her face. "It would be too much work to get the boys here."

"Are you sure?" His voice was heavy and laden with disappointment.

"I'm sure."

He didn't beg or plead. He didn't try to convince her or tell her all the reasons she should be with him on Christmas. Instead, he turned off the engine, exited the car and walked around the vehicle to open the door for her, leaving many things unsaid.

Which was exactly what she wanted. The less they said, the less she could regret.

It had been a slow week for Jacob, waiting for the Ashers' first annual Christmas fundraiser on Saturday. The formal affair would be held in their home, and the profits from ticket sales, silent auction items and donations would go directly to the nonprofit organization they had formed to help widows and orphans in Timber Falls. Jacob had been on their board of directors since its inception about six months ago, and he was excited to attend.

Especially because he would escort Kate.

"Daddy." Maggie put on her boots in the front foyer. Her brow wrinkled as she inspected his appearance. "Are you too fancy?"

Jacob inspected his appearance in the hall mirror and shook his head. "Not for tonight's event." He hadn't worn a tuxedo since his wedding day and felt a little conspicuous in it as he pulled on his long black coat. "All the men will be wearing tuxedos at the Ashers' home tonight."

"And what about the ladies?" She took her coat off the hook and pulled it onto her arms. "Will they wear tuxedos?"

"No." He smiled and helped her with the second sleeve. "They'll wear gowns."

"Gowns?" Maggie continued to frown. "Like my princess dress-up clothes?"

"Not quite."

"Will Kate wear a gown?"

"Yes. I believe she and Mrs. Asher went shopping yesterday."

Maggie squealed with glee as she pulled a knitted cap over her blond hair and then put on her mittens. "Are the church ladies going to babysit me tonight?"

"They'll be at the Ashers' home, so you'll have a couple teenagers as your babysitters."

Jacob grabbed his keys from the calling card dish on the side table and opened the door for Maggie, thankful for her chatter, which helped keep his nerves at bay.

Maggie stepped onto the front porch while Jacob turned off the lights. He took her hand as they crossed the street to Kate's house.

Soft snowflakes drifted down from the sky,

illuminated by the globes from the streetlight on the corner. As they walked, clouds of frosty air billowed from their mouths and the snow crunched under their feet.

"Is Kate your girlfriend, Daddy?" Maggie asked.

"No."

She was pensive for a moment. "If she was, I would like that."

Jacob couldn't deny that he would like that, too. "You wouldn't be sad that I had a girlfriend, and that one day you could have a new mommy?"

"Not if it was Kate." Her simple answer spoke a magnitude about Kate LeClair. Maggie didn't give her approval often.

They walked around the snowdrifts, hand in hand.

"You need to prepare yourself for when they leave," Jacob told his daughter. "Kate is planning to take the boys with her on tour."

Maggie looked up at Jacob, her eyes huge under the lamplight. "She's taking the triplets away from me?"

"She's not taking them away from you— just with her." His disappointment over her announcement the other night still stung as fresh as it had when she'd told him. "She has a job and needs to return to it before Christmas."

"Her play?"

"Yes. She'll rejoin her cast when she reaches Minneapolis."

"That's not too far away."

"No, it's not. But she'll leave Minneapolis a week or so after that and go somewhere farther away."

"Can we go see her in the play?"

The thought had crossed Jacob's mind, but he wasn't sure *Les Misérables* was appropriate for his seven-year-old. "I don't think so, Mags. The tickets are expensive."

"That's all I want for Christmas," she said, pulling on his hand and begging. "Please."

He shook his head. "Let's not talk about this. I said no."

She pouted, but they had arrived at Kate's house, so he pushed open the door, knowing they were expected, and didn't bother to knock.

The moment he and Maggie stepped over the threshold, Kate appeared at the top of the stairs in a simple yet stunning evening gown. It was black, with a tight top and a skirt that flared out at the waist, going all the way down to her toes. Her hair was up and off her shoulders, and she wore a long shimmering necklace with matching earrings.

She met his gaze and held it for a heartbeat, and then descended to the foyer.

Jacob couldn't find his voice and was thankful his daughter was oohing and aahing over Kate's appearance.

"You look so pretty, Kate," Maggie said.

"Thank you." Kate hugged Maggie close.

"You look like a princess." Maggie's eyes were bright. "Daddy said you wouldn't look like one."

"That's not what I said, Mags." He'd finally found his voice, heat gathering around his collar at his daughter's mistaken comment.

Kate looked at Jacob with a little hesitation and he knew he needed to make amends quickly.

"You are breathtaking, Kate." He took her hand in his, afraid his face and voice and eyes would tell her too much. "And I agree with Maggie. You do look like a princess."

Kate looked down at her hand, which was nestled in his, and then she let her eyes trail up his tuxedo until her gaze was fixed on his again. "You look—" She paused and shook her head in appreciation. "Amazing."

Her compliment went straight to his heart and he let it linger there. "A tux can transform almost any man."

Her cheeks and eyes glowed as she admired him. "You look just as amazing in a pair of worn jeans and a sweatshirt."

Not for the first time, he thought back to the

conversation he'd had with his dad on Thanksgiving. His dad had asked if Kate was interested in him and Jacob had said no—but there were moments like this one that his heart suggested otherwise. He longed to know—but even as the thought took shape, he knew it wouldn't change anything. He was a simple pastor, living in a small town, in a house he didn't own, with a very modest income. He could never offer Kate the kind of life she was accustomed to. His salary hardly allowed him to travel, and when he did, it was to pastoral conferences. How could he ask her to give up Broadway? And a national tour? She'd worked so hard for the things she had—who was he to ask her to set it all aside and join his humble life in Timber Falls?

"The babysitters are in the toy room," Kate said to Maggie. "I've already said goodbye to the boys and given the sitters some instructions. Do you want to join them?"

"Sure!" Maggie reached up and gave Jacob a hug, and then ran off to join the others.

Kate went to the hook and lifted off a long wool coat. Jacob took it from her and helped her into it.

"I have a request," she said, as she turned to face him. They were close—very close—and he could smell the sweet scent of her perfume.

"Anything."

"Could we walk to the party?"

He raised his eyebrows. "It's several blocks away."

"I know." She buttoned up her coat and then lifted the hem of her gown to reveal a pair of snow boots. "I came prepared."

He laughed, never expecting to see bulky boots under her elegant gown.

"I have my heels in my bag." She lifted up a purse to show him. "It's just so beautiful outside and I miss walking. I used to walk everywhere in New York."

"If you want to walk, then let's walk." It would be chilly, but with Kate by his side, he was certain he wouldn't feel the cold.

She pulled gloves onto her hands, wrapped a scarf around her neck and then opened the door.

He followed her outside, closing the door behind them, and offered her his arm. "I'd feel better about us walking on ice and snow if we could offer each other a little support."

She smiled and wrapped her arm through his, drawing close to his side. She looked up at him and the familiarity and adoration he felt for her expanded in his chest. It warmed him all the way to his toes.

Even if he couldn't keep Kate for always, at least he had her by his side for now.

He reveled in her nearness, drawing her

closer to him. "How have you grown so important to me in such a short time, Kate LeClair?" he asked quietly, the words slipping from his mouth with little thought.

Her smile was soft and comfortable, full of affection. She leaned into him as they started down her walkway toward the street. "I've wondered the same thing about you," she said gently. "You make me feel safe and comfortable—something I haven't felt very often in my life." They walked past the church and turned onto Broadway. "You've become very important to me—and the boys—too."

They walked in silence for several minutes and Jacob tried to capture the beauty of the moment, wanting to hold on to it forever. Snowflakes danced on the air, Christmas lights twinkled from homes and trees and stores, and people shuffled from shop to shop, buying Christmas gifts after work.

"It's less than a week before the Christmas program," Kate said, breaking the silence. "And then a day after that I'll rejoin the cast in Minneapolis."

Jacob's heart constricted at the thought.

"Maggie is doing a marvelous job as the angel in the program." Breath plumed out of her mouth as she spoke. "I'm very pleased with the whole cast."

"You're doing a great job directing them. I've heard nothing but praise from the parents."

She squeezed his arm in response.

They walked down Broadway, neither one rushing or trying to go faster than necessary. Kate's hem brushed the snow, leaving a trail in her wake.

"Jacob, there's something I'd like to tell you." Kate paused under a green historic streetlight. The large globes and twinkling lights on the wreath above her head reflected in her eyes, revealing the deep anguish within.

"What is it?" He frowned and put his hand on her upper arm, wanting to take away whatever it was that gave her such pain.

She studied him for a moment, and then wrapped her arm through his again. "I think we need to keep walking while I tell you."

His pulse pumped harder as he waited for her to tell him whatever it was that made her look so troubled. They turned left onto Main Street and had about five blocks to go.

"I know I don't have to tell you this—and I honestly don't even know why I am, except—" She swallowed and looked away from him. "I want you to know who I am. You've become such a good friend, I feel like this is something I would tell a friend—or my pastor."

A friend. Her pastor. He tried to deny the disappointment he felt at the titles she had given him. It was just as he'd suspected—though the truth was more crushing than he wanted to acknowledge. He loved Kate—was in love with Kate, if he were honest with himself. It was just as his dad had said at Thanksgiving. He just knew—had known for a long time—that Kate was different from the other women he'd met. There was something that drew him to her and he felt safe offering her his heart. They hadn't known each other for long, but what he did know about her, he liked immensely.

But if her friendship was all she could offer, then it would have to be enough. He couldn't lose her altogether.

And as her pastor, it wasn't right to ask her for more.

"I'm here to listen—as your friend—and as your pastor."

She took a deep breath, blowing out a fog of air from her lips. "I have a daughter."

Jacob's feet stumbled and he came to a stop near the entrance to Basswood Park. "A what?"

She pulled away from him, her back against the park sign. "A daughter."

His mind spun with so many questions he couldn't focus. "Where? When?"

"I had her when I was eighteen." She looked down at her gloved hands, shame and embarrassment heavy on her shoulders. "I had been dating my boyfriend for almost a year. He was also in theater at my high school. When I found out I was pregnant, he told me he didn't want the child—or me—and left."

Jacob closed his eyes, pain filling his heart as he imagined Kate as a teenager facing such horrible rejection.

"My mom told me I couldn't keep the baby. She was so ashamed of me." Kate finally looked up at Jacob, tears glistening in her eyes. "She told me I couldn't tell Tabby—or anyone else— so that's when I stopped writing to my cousin. I dropped out of high school and worked a full-time job. After I gave birth to the baby and gave her up for adoption, I left the very next day for New York City." The tears spilled down her cheeks. "I made a new life for myself and worked tirelessly, night and day, to get to where I'm at. But not one day goes by that I don't think about my little girl or wonder where she is. Every time I'm on stage and see a girl about her age in the audience, I wonder if it's her—a-and if she's proud of me." She shook her head, the tears falling freely now.

Jacob had spent hours counseling people— but never had he felt so heartbroken or so invested in their pain. He took Kate into his arms and held her as she cried, running his hand down her back, whispering soothing words to her weary soul.

"How old would she be?" he asked quietly.

"Maggie's age."

Jacob held her tighter, aware of how hard it must have been to spend so much time with Maggie this past month, knowing her own daughter was the same age.

"I'm sorry, Jacob." She pulled away and wiped at her cheeks with her gloved hands.

"Sorry?" He removed a tear she had missed. "Why?"

"Because I shouldn't burden you with my problems—yet, that's all I've done since I met you."

"Kate." He put his hands on her shoulders and looked deep into her eyes. "I want to shoulder the burden—not only is it my job, but I care about you. Very much."

She studied his face for a moment, her eyes still watery. "Can God forgive me for what I've done?" she whispered.

"Have you asked Him to?"

"About a thousand times."

"Once is enough." He drew her into his arms again. "The book of First John says if we confess our sins, He is faithful and just and will forgive us. It's time to let go of the guilt and shame."

They held each other for a long time, the snow falling all around them. Finally, she pulled away.

"I'm going to look horrible when we arrive at the party." She tried to laugh as she wiped at her cheeks again.

He couldn't hide the admiration or love from his voice. "I don't think anything could make you look horrible."

Her smile was wobbly as she took a deep cleansing breath. "Thank you, Jacob. You have no idea how good it feels to talk to you."

He had an idea—because he felt the same way about talking to her.

Chapter Twelve

The Asher mansion was ablaze with light and merriment as they walked up the long driveway. Kate's feet were cold, but her heart was warm as she arrived at the party beside Jacob. She still couldn't get over how handsome he looked, or how good it had felt to finally tell him about her past. She hadn't been sure how he would respond, and a part of her had worried that he would condemn her or banish her from his friendship. Thankfully, he had done neither, and assured her that she was forgiven—but, more importantly, he'd shown her that she was loved.

The moment they entered the Asher home, she excused herself and went into the powder room to freshen up her makeup. She was certain she'd look like a swollen tomato, but was pleasantly surprised to find her face glowing—

whether from the cold or the freedom that came from unburdening her past, she didn't know.

"Kate!" Joy called to her from across the foyer when Kate exited the powder room. "I was wondering when you two were coming."

Jacob stood next to Joy and her husband, Chase. The young couple were striking together, and looked so in love—Kate couldn't help but smile for her friend's happiness. Joy's hunter green gown accentuated her growing stomach and made her look radiant.

"You look lovely," Joy said with a quick hug for Kate. "I was telling Chase that I was a little envious that the first gown you tried on fit you perfectly—when it took me three fittings and two seamstresses to look halfway presentable tonight."

"Don't mind her," Chase said to Joy. "She knows she looks amazing."

Joy grinned and kissed her husband's cheek. "That's why I married you."

"Your home is gorgeous," Kate said to Joy, admiring the festive decorations. Live pine garland graced every conceivable surface, with red ribbons, holly and poinsettias mixed in. Already, at least a hundred people milled about the rooms. Live music drifted from the music room and the air was filled with the delectable aroma of holiday food.

"People have begun to dance," Joy said to Jacob. "Grab a drink and something to eat in the dining room and then invite Kate to dance."

Jacob met Kate's gaze, a question in their depths. "Would you like to?"

"I would love to dance."

The evening was a wonderful success. Kate loved meeting more community members and seeing those she already knew. The church ladies moved around in a tight knot, rarely straying from one another's side, their husbands trailing after them quietly. The food, catered in for the event, but overseen by Mrs. Thompson, was delicious.

Everywhere Kate looked, people were happy and carefree, celebrating the season. The men looked handsome, the women lovely and the house magnificent.

It was another Timber Falls moment Kate hoped she would never forget.

Jacob and Kate danced several times, laughing and talking like old friends. More than once, Kate noticed the sideways glances of the church ladies—and several others—and knew she and Jacob were giving a convincing performance.

The only thing was—they weren't performing. Kate had never felt more like herself than she did in Jacob's company. It wasn't hard to be with him—on the contrary, the thought of leaving him and Timber Falls in eight days was the only thing that put a pall over the evening.

Before too long, it was time to leave.

"Must you go so soon?" Joy asked Kate, as Jacob helped her slip on her coat.

"We walked," Kate said, "and I promised the babysitters we wouldn't be out late, so we should leave now."

"Walked?" Chase frowned. "Car troubles, Jacob?"

Jacob smiled and nodded at Kate. "It was at the lady's request."

"Chase can give you a ride home," Joy said. "He wouldn't mind."

"Of course not," Chase responded.

Kate shook her head. "Thank you, but I'd like to walk back—if it's okay with Jacob."

"I'm at your beck and call," he said with a wink.

Joy hugged Kate and promised to come by soon for a longer visit.

They left the mansion and found themselves back in the snow. It was falling a little heavier now, though there was hardly any wind, making it a pleasant night for another walk.

"My heart is full," Kate said to Jacob.

"Did you have a good time?"

"I can't remember a more wonderful time."

"That's high praise coming from a Broadway actress."

She wrapped her arm through his again, loving his strong, steady presence at her side.

They walked in silence for most of the way, Kate deep in thought about her time in Timber Falls and everything that awaited her and the boys on tour. It wouldn't be easy, but she'd find a way to make it work, and hopefully, after the tour ended, she could land a role in the city, so she wouldn't have to travel again.

The streets were quieter now that the stores had closed. Timber Falls slumbered in the winter night, and Kate marveled that the town could be so still.

"New York City never sleeps," she mused, as they drew closer to the church and her home. "I feel so safe and comfortable in Timber Falls."

Jacob led her across the snowy street to the corner of Third and Broadway. The church was dark, but Kate's house was still lit up. She had put a small tree in the living room window, even though she knew she and the boys wouldn't be there for Christmas. It twinkled now, inviting her home, and she was thankful she had gone to the trouble.

They rounded the corner of the church and Jacob came to a sudden halt, drawing Kate to a stop beside him.

"What in the world?" Jacob dropped Kate's arm and started jogging through the parking lot behind the church.

Kate's gaze shot to the direction he was running and that's when she saw what had pulled him away.

In the shadows, someone was spray painting the side of her garage.

Thankful for her boots, Kate quickly followed Jacob and arrived at the scene of the crime as Jacob grabbed the arm of the young man who tried to flee toward his silver Audi, which was parked behind Kate's garage in the alley.

"Let me go!" Aaron Johnson said. "You can't treat me this way!"

"Keep it down, or you'll wake up the whole neighborhood." Jacob started to haul the teenager toward the church.

"I don't care if I do. Then they'll see how you're manhandling me."

"Aaron, you're in no position to make threats right now." Jacob dug in his pocket and pulled out a set of keys. "Kate, can you open the church door? I'm afraid if I let him go, he'll try to run."

Aaron tried to yank his arm away from Jacob, but Jacob held him fast.

"What do you think you're going to do to me?" Aaron asked.

"I'm calling your father—and the other elders of the church. It's time we confronted this situation."

"What situation?"

"You know what I'm talking about."

Kate fumbled with the keys, but she was finally able to unlock the door and push it open.

Jacob hauled Aaron over the threshold and Kate followed close behind, switching on the lights as she went.

They walked down the hall to Jacob's office. "Sit," he said to Aaron. "And don't do anything you'll regret."

Aaron sat on the chair, his shoulders slumped, anger and disrespect radiating off him.

Jacob went to the phone and made several calls. Kate knew when he was talking to Aaron's dad, because the voice on the other end could be heard through the receiver.

They sat in silence for about ten minutes before the elders started to arrive, some of them in tuxedos, having been called away from the Ashers' party.

One by one, they came into Jacob's office, until Aaron's father finally arrived about twenty minutes after Jacob had made the call.

"What's the meaning of this?" Rick Johnson asked the room at large the moment he entered.

"Maybe you should ask your son." Jacob

leaned against the edge of his desk, his arms and ankles crossed.

"I asked you," Rick said to Jacob. "What is this about?"

Jacob's face held no condemnation as he looked at Rick—but Kate was surprised at the anger simmering under the surface of his self-control. "Miss LeClair and I had just returned from the Ashers' party when we found Aaron spray-painting Kate's garage."

"That's absurd." Rick shook his head, his comb-over flopping with the motion.

"Look at his fingers," Jacob said. "They still have red spray paint on them."

The six other elders watched the scene carefully, though no one spoke.

"Is it true?" Rick finally asked his son. "Were you spray-painting Miss LeClair's garage?"

Aaron looked down at his hands, his head hanging low. "Yes, sir."

Defeat wrinkled Rick's brow. "Why?"

"To make you happy." Aaron didn't bother to look at his dad.

"Happy? By vandalizing her property? What would be the point?"

"To convince her that it's not a safe place to live."

Kate stood in the foreground of the room, not wanting to be present, but knowing she had a duty to be there since it was her home that was affected.

"What made you think that?" Rick asked Aaron.

Aaron just shrugged.

Jacob sighed. "Did you do the other damage to Miss LeClair's property, Aaron?"

"Yes, sir."

Jacob glanced up and met Kate's gaze before looking at the other elders. "I think it's safe to say that there should be a consequence for Aaron's behavior."

"Don't you dare presume to discipline my child," Rick said.

"I wasn't presuming—I just thought—"

"My son is only trying to do what you have failed to do, which is make Miss LeClair see the foolishness of keeping that house."

Kate bit her lip, hating to be spoken about right in front of her.

"I have failed at nothing." Jacob continued to cross his arms. "Kate knows we're interested in her house, and she's going to make the best decision for her and the boys."

"How can anything other than selling the house be the best decision?" Rick turned to Kate, taking her off guard.

She jumped at the sudden attention.

"Do you know how selfish you're being?"

Rick asked her. "It's God's will that you sell your home to us. You're being disobedient by holding on to it."

Kate's mouth slipped open.

Jacob uncrossed his arms and stood, his back rigid. "You're out of line, Rick. Who are you to speak for God?"

"Who am I not to?" Rick asked. "As the head elder, I know what's best for this church."

"Accusing Kate of disobeying God and making her feel unwelcome is not what is best for this church."

"So now you're speaking for God?"

"No. I'm speaking for myself." Color filled Jacob's cheeks and Kate stood quietly, surprised at his passion. "I cannot sit here and let you represent this church when all you're doing is harming it."

"Everyone needs to calm down," Mr. Jenkins said, raising his hands for attention. "Things are getting out of control—"

"I will not be told to calm down," Rick said to Mr. Jenkins. "As the head elder—"

"Maybe it's time we address that issue," said another elder, one Kate didn't know. "Rick, you've been nothing but a bully from the moment you were elected, and I, for one, am tired of it."

Several of the elders nodded their agreement.

"I wouldn't be a bully if our pastor did his job." Rick wiped spittle from his chin. "I want that school, and I'll do whatever it takes to get it."

"Jacob goes above and beyond his call of duty," Mr. Jenkins said. "We've never had a more dedicated pastor at Timber Falls Community Church."

Several agreed.

"If that's true," Rick argued, "then why don't we have a school built?"

"Because of matters beyond our control," a third elder spoke up to Rick while glancing at Kate. "Miss LeClair's family has been through a horrible tragedy, and instead of easing that burden, like Jacob has been doing, you're only adding more pressure on her."

Kate wanted to fade into the background but had nowhere to go.

"Since we're all present," Mr. Jenkins said. "I'd like to call a special meeting to order, with one item on our agenda. Who is in favor of letting Rick Johnson remain on the elder board?"

No one spoke.

"Who is in favor of removing him from the board?"

Everyone said aye.

"Motion carries." Mr. Jenkins straightened his shoulders. "Mr. Johnson, it's time you took your son home. You'll be hearing from us regarding his punishment, which will more than likely include repainting Miss LeClair's garage and reimbursing her for the cost to fix her fence and garage window."

Rick's face was red and his eyes bulged. He grabbed Aaron by the back of his coat and hauled him out of the office without another word.

Kate simply stared, not wanting to draw attention, afraid that everything that had just transpired was somehow her fault.

If only she'd agreed to sell the house—none of this would have happened. What did she really need with it, anyway? It was just a house—and she didn't even know if the boys would want it someday. Was it right to saddle them with something they might not want, but would feel obligated to accept, just because Kate had said so?

"I'm sorry things had to come to this," Mr. Jenkins said to the others in the room. "It's getting late. Why don't we meet back here on Monday evening and discuss how we want to move forward?"

The men gathered their coats and said their goodbyes, many of them stopping to apologize to Kate on their way out.

When Kate and Jacob were alone, he suddenly looked tired.

"I'm sorry, Kate." He shook his head. "I feel like all of this is my fault."

"Then join the club, because I was thinking the same thing."

"You? How could it be your fault?"

She let out a sigh. "I should have just agreed to sell the house right away. What do I need with it?"

He frowned. "It's your home—your family home. You shouldn't have to make any excuses or need any reason to keep the house. It's yours—and not the church's, just because Rick Johnson says so."

"It would make your job a lot easier if I sold it, wouldn't it?"

Jacob rubbed his forehead and shook his head. "It doesn't matter. You need to do what's right for you."

Kate knew what would be right for her—making Jacob's job easier.

Ten minutes later, Jacob left Kate's house after dropping her off. Maggie was already asleep and Kate said she'd bring her to church in the morning.

So Jacob entered his house alone. The old place creaked and moaned as he closed the front door. Without bothering to turn on the overhead lights, he walked into the formal front parlor and plugged in the Christmas tree he and Maggie had decorated the previous week.

The white lights glowed, filling the room with the soft ambiance of Christmas.

Jacob took a seat on the stiff sofa and stared at the tree. He hadn't felt uncomfortable in his tuxedo until this very moment, but didn't have the heart or the energy to go upstairs and change.

Several ornaments caught his attention, each one making him recall a different time and place. Some were from his childhood, some were from the first years he and Laura had been married and others had been added by Maggie. Her homemade Popsicle-stick stars and clothespin reindeers usually made him smile.

But tonight, very little could make him smile.

He'd been appalled at Rick's and Aaron's behaviors—not only because they represented Timber Falls but because they represented the church. Jacob had suddenly become aware that he had been trying really hard to get Kate to love the town and church community, thinking maybe they could convince her to stay.

But in reality, he had wanted her to stay because of him—regardless of where he lived. He'd been hiding behind the church and community, because he had been afraid he wasn't enough and that she'd need something else to persuade her to stay.

The truth was that none of it was enough. He saw it in her eyes tonight. She would sell the house to the church, probably out of guilt, and then she would have nothing tying her to the community any longer.

Jacob couldn't tell her what to do—especially because he represented the church and knew their desire to build a school—but he also couldn't sit back and let Kate give up a tangible connection to her family roots.

It might cost him his job, but if she offered to sell the house, he would be ready with a solid argument of why she shouldn't. Not only so she could keep a connection to the town her ancestors helped to build—but because the town could keep a connection to Kate, too.

His heart ached when he thought about her leaving and knew he only had eight more days. Eight days to savor her friendship, to make more memories…and to convince her to stay, because of him.

Chapter Thirteen

Kate sat on the floor in the boys' toy room, laughing at Carter as he pulled himself onto a chair from the small table and dunked the basket into the hoop. She clapped for him and he grinned at her, and then climbed off the chair, grabbed the ball and did it all over again.

"Mamamama." Aiken toddled up to her with his favorite book and plopped himself into her lap. Bryce sat nearby stacking blocks, one on top the other, and then knocked them down with a laugh.

Kate wrapped her arms around Aiken and kissed his little head. Her gaze wandered out of the toy room and into the living room where nothing but the couch and a rocking chair remained with the Christmas tree.

The house echoed with the laughter of the

boys. It reverberated off the wood floors, the empty walls and the bare rooms.

Everything had been tossed, donated or stored. In between rehearsals at the church and caring for the boys, Kate had managed to go through the entire house from the basement up to the attic. Joy had come by several times to help, as had Maggie, who was surprisingly talented at organization. Slowly, but surely, Kate had hauled away the boxes to Goodwill or the storage unit she had rented on the outskirts of town. In a year, when she was done with *Les Misérables*, she would return to collect her things to bring to New York.

But, for now, she would enjoy watching the boys play with the few toys she had kept out for them.

Tomorrow would be the Christmas program and the next day she would put the boys' suitcases in the back of the minivan and drive them to Minneapolis where she'd join the cast. Before she left, she would hand Jacob an envelope with her wishes concerning the house. For days, she'd been trying to compose the note to him in her mind but hadn't known how to sum up everything in a simple card.

She would give the house to the church for them to use however they'd like.

She didn't want to say anything to him or the

elders until the very last minute, because she didn't want to cause a fuss. They would probably want to make a big deal about the donation, but she'd rather not draw that kind of attention. She wanted to leave Timber Falls as quietly as possible and other than Jacob, Maggie and Joy, she wouldn't say goodbye.

It would be too hard.

The doorbell rang and Kate kissed Aiken again and then set him aside. "I'll come back and read to you in a little bit."

He didn't seem to mind the intrusion and picked up the toy lying next to him, forgetting his book where it lay.

Kate looked out the front window and didn't recognize the SUV parked near the curb, nor did she recognize the lady who stood at her front door.

"May I help you?" she asked when she opened the door.

The woman wore a long wool coat and had gleaming white teeth behind bright red lipstick. Her brown hair was styled in a tight twist. "I'm Constance Mayweather." She extended a business card. "I'm a realtor with New Horizons Realty and I would love to talk to you about your house."

"I'm sorry," Kate said. "It's not for sale."

"Well, hear me out." She put up her hand, her

long red fingernails just as bright as her lipstick. "I'm aware that the church needs this property to add on a school."

Kate nodded, not surprised that this woman knew all about it—everyone did.

"I think it would be a travesty to see this house torn down," Constance said.

It was something Kate was trying hard not to think about.

"I have a couple who have been looking for an older home in town, one similar to yours—but with no success."

"I'm sorry." Kate shook her head, not wanting to make this woman work any harder than necessary to try to convince her.

"I have found a plot of land near the river and proposed to this couple that, if I could get you to sell them the house, they could move it off this spot and onto the river property." She grinned, revealing her gleaming teeth. "Is that something you'd consider?"

Kate's heartbeat picked up its pace and she clutched the doorknob. "The house can be moved?"

"With a little bit of work, some expenses and a few permits, yes."

If the house were moved—and spared—then the church would have an empty lot to add on their school. It seemed ideal. Was this God's answer to her prayers?

Kate opened the door wider and motioned Constance to come in. "I would very much consider this offer."

"Wonderful!" Constance pulled a folder out of her briefcase. "The couple has sent me with an offer and a purchase agreement, if you are ready to sign on the dotted line."

It didn't matter to Kate how much money they offered. She would donate the money from the sale of the house, along with the land, to the church.

"Why don't you come into the kitchen?" Kate asked. "I'll make some coffee and we can discuss the details."

"That sounds lovely."

Two hours later, after Kate had called her lawyer and had him look over the purchase agreement, which the realtor emailed to him, the deal was signed and finished. The closing date would be in two weeks, though Kate would have to sign the title over to them from the road.

Everything had been so effortless. There was no striving, no uncertainty, no obstacles. It all fit into place, feeling as if it was meant to be. Kate couldn't deny that God's hand had been in the whole affair and she thanked Him now for answering her prayers. The house wouldn't be bulldozed. Jacob would get his school. And Kate could leave Timber Falls, knowing she had no unfinished business.

At least, where the house was concerned.

Her heart felt otherwise.

Now, Kate sat in the toy room with the boys again, unsure what to do with herself. Everything was packed, the Christmas program was ready to go, the set had been assembled and the costumes had been made.

"What will we do with ourselves until Maggie gets here?" she asked the boys.

"Maymay," Bryce said while clapping his hands, his name for Maggie sounding sweet on his lips.

"You'll miss MayMay, won't you?" she asked the little boy. "All of us will miss MayMay."

And her daddy.

Kate had been so busy this past week, she'd hardly seen Jacob, other than briefly at church and when he came to pick Maggie up after work. The church ladies were no longer bringing her meals, so she had no excuse to invite him in for supper.

They saw each other in passing when Kate was at the church for rehearsals, but she was so preoccupied with her production, she hadn't taken much time to talk to him.

Kate's phone rang in her back pocket, so she pulled it out.

It was Jacob.

"Hello," she said, as she stood and went to the window.

He sat at his desk, facing her house.

"Hi, Kate."

"I was just thinking about you."

"That's funny. I was just thinking about you, too."

She longed to know what he was thinking, but would never ask.

"Do you have everything you need for the Christmas program tomorrow night?" he asked.

Was that why he'd been thinking about her?

"Yes. Everyone's ready to go. The kids will arrive a couple hours early and we'll have one more dress rehearsal before the real thing."

There was a moment's hesitation, and then he asked, "Does that mean you're free tonight?"

She hadn't been alone with Jacob since the night of the Ashers' party, and though she saw him on a regular basis, she missed him.

"I am free. What do you have in mind?"

"I've already spoken to Mrs. Caruthers and Mrs. Anderson and they volunteered to watch the children if you agreed to go out with me."

Go out with him? As in, on a date? Surely, he couldn't mean a date.

She swallowed and toyed with the lace curtain. "Where did you want to go?"

He hesitated and then said, "I want it to be a surprise."

Her stomach filled with butterflies at the prospect of spending the evening with Jacob, and despite her better judgment that she should keep space between them so it wouldn't be as hard to say goodbye, she knew it was too late for that and found herself nodding. "I'd love to."

"Good." She could hear the smile in his voice. "I'll let the church ladies know to come about seven and I'll drop Maggie off. Does that sound okay?"

"It sounds great—but—" She hated to bring up something that she knew would be difficult to discuss. "I've moved a lot of things out of the house already."

"Oh."

"And I had planned to leave Timber Falls quietly. If the church ladies know the house is empty, then they'll know I'm leaving soon and everyone will make a big fuss."

"And you hate goodbyes."

"I do." Especially the one she would have to share with him and Maggie.

"Do you want them to come to my house? I know it's more work for you to get the boys out the door—"

"That probably wouldn't work, either, since the boys lie down to bed at eight and I would hate to wake them, bundle them up and get them across the road to their beds. The last thing you'd want is for them to have a sleepover." She wanted desperately to make this outing work, but she couldn't think of a way. Disappointment stung her eyes and she was afraid she might cry.

Neither one spoke for a moment.

"I hate to think you're leaving in two days," Jacob said quietly.

Kate couldn't answer, the tears hovering. Why were goodbyes so hard?

"How about I hire the teenagers who babysat on the night of the Ashers' party?" Jacob asked suddenly. "There's a far greater chance that they could care less about the lack of furniture in your house. We'll give them some money and they can order a pizza."

Kate's heart picked up its pace again. "That could work."

"I'll call them right now."

"Thank you."

"Be ready by seven," he said. "And dress warm."

"I will."

Jacob hung up the phone and Kate did the same. She moved away from the window, feeling lighter than she had in days. "I'm going out with the preacher tonight."

The boys glanced at her, but none of them responded, leaving Kate to enjoy the moment alone.

Until she remembered that it would be the last outing she'd have with Jacob—and the beginning of their goodbye.

"Where are you taking me?" Kate asked for the third time since Jacob had picked her up.

"You'll see soon enough." Jacob laughed at her pursed lips and calculating eyes. "You don't like surprises, do you?"

"They're almost as bad as goodbyes."

Jacob had told himself that he wouldn't think about Kate's imminent departure tonight. Instead, he would live fully in the moment and put the past—and the future—out of his head.

He pulled into the Ashers' long driveway, candles in white paper bags lighting their path in the winter darkness.

"We're going to see Chase and Joy?" Kate asked.

"No."

She frowned. "Then why are we at their house?"

"You'll see." He shook his head. "You're a very impatient woman."

Kate smiled at him—one of those blinding, gorgeous smiles that he'd come to love.

He drove past the Ashers' home and down

the hill to the carriage house. Several other vehicles were parked along the road with more candles illuminating a path from the parking area, around the carriage house and down to the pond just beyond.

Kate sat quietly in the passenger seat, but her eyes asked a dozen questions.

He just laughed and got out of the car. Opening the trunk, he pulled out two pairs of ice skates and brought them to the passenger door.

"Have you ever been skating before?" he asked her.

"Skating?" Her eyebrows rose together. "Not since I was a kid." She stepped out of the car. "Where did you get skates for me?"

"Joy. She told me you two had the same size of feet—and she knew that from shopping with you the other day."

"So Joy was in on this?"

"Of course. Who do you think told me about the skating pond?" He indicated the candlelit path. "They cleared the ice this year for the first time and have invited the community to use it for skating."

She followed him down the path, through the wooded area on the side of the hill and to the pond. More candles, inside white paper bags, rimmed the edges of the pond where a dozen people were skating.

Jacob led Kate into the warming house and helped her put on her skates.

"It's been almost fifteen years since I skated," Kate said with a warning in her voice. "I might need some help."

Jacob grinned as he knelt in front of her and tied the laces of her skates. "That's what I'm here for."

When they were done, he offered his hand, which she took, and he led her back outside to the pond. Her steps were unsteady, but he appreciated her willingness to try.

Stars sparkled above and a light wind whispered across the frozen water. The sound of slicing blades against ice mingled with the soft laughter from the skaters.

"Ready?" he asked.

She nodded, her focus on her feet.

He stepped onto the ice and held her hand as she followed him.

They started to glide, a little wobbly at first, and then their movements evened out as they made a big circle around the pond, his left arm around her back, his right hand holding hers.

Cold wind nipped at Jacob's nose and cheeks, but he didn't mind. He loved watching Kate smile as she skated beside him, her laughter and smiles warming him through.

She hadn't let him go, even when she'd become confident on the blades. As they glided together, neither one spoke. There were so many things he wanted to tell her—so many things on his mind and heart—but he held back. He wanted her to love him—to stay—but he knew better than anyone that he had nothing to offer.

And more than that, there was still a part of Jacob that felt guilty for pushing Laura to do something she hadn't wanted to do. That's why Jacob hadn't pressured Kate to sell or to stay in Timber Falls—and why he hesitated to tell her he was in love with her now. He couldn't be the cause of Kate missing out on her best life—and staying in Timber Falls to be his wife might not be the best thing for her—even if it would be the best thing for him.

"You're quieter than usual tonight." Kate looked at him in the soft light of the candles, her voice gentle. Her eyes, which were luminous and beautiful, drew him in, just as they always did.

"There's a lot on my mind tonight," he said just as gently.

She nestled in closer to his side and pleasure raced through Jacob. As Kate leaned into him, he held her tight, never wanting her to leave his side again. The weight of his dreams felt like a millstone around his heart tonight. Why did he want something that seemed so impossible?

Despite his better judgment, he could no longer keep his feelings to himself. "Kate."

They had skated to the opposite side of the pond, far away from the carriage house and the other skaters. A canopy of trees enclosed this portion of the pond, shielding them from the wind and offering a bit more privacy. The candles burned brighter here, sending flickering shadows dancing on the ice.

He drew her to a stop, his heart pounding as she glided around to face him, a question in her eyes.

His arms were still around her, and her skates touched the tips of his, but she didn't pull away. Instead, she looked up at him with curiosity.

"Kate," he said again, his breath frosty on the cold night air. He shook his head, a thousand thoughts clamoring to be spoken at once, but only one that said it all. "I don't want you to leave."

She closed her eyes briefly and pressed her lips together. When she met his gaze again, regret rimmed her eyes. "I can't stay, Jacob."

"Why not?"

"There are so many reasons I must go."

"But there are so many reasons to stay."

"Are there?" She studied his face closely, as if searching for an answer to an unspoken question. "Why should I stay?"

"Because I want you to." He swallowed hard. "I've never met anyone like you. You've turned my world upside down and I don't think it will ever return to normal again."

A soft crinkle marred the space between her brows as she listened to him. "Jacob, you're good and kind—and your heart is bigger than any I've ever known." She put her hand on his chest. "I've never met anyone like you before, either. You've made me feel welcome and cared for—you've made me feel like Timber Falls is home."

His heart began to pound harder when he heard the shift in the tone of her voice and knew she was pulling away from him.

"I care for you—" she choked on the word, emotion thick in her voice "—very much. But I don't belong here—I never have, and I'm afraid if I stayed, everyone else would come to realize that, as well."

She was a successful actress. Her life was on the stage. Just as he'd always feared, she could never settle for a simple life in a small town. Her calling was bigger and grander than his. He wasn't bitter or angry—he'd accepted long ago that he would never have a glamorous lifestyle. He didn't blame Kate for not wanting what he had to offer. He'd known it all along.

But it still hurt.

He dropped his gaze, and let her go, putting space between them. He didn't want her to see the sting from her rejection in his eyes—didn't want her to know he loved her. He probably wasn't the first man to fall in love with her. She probably faced this all the time. She was a public figure—and he'd been a fool to think she could possibly fall for him. Embarrassment overwhelmed him, but he didn't want her to see it, either.

She pulled off her glove and reached up to place her hand on his cheek. "Jacob, the last thing I want to do is hurt you." She shook her head. "That's why I can't stay."

Her skin was warm against his cold cheek and he had to force down the desire to press into it. "How could you ever hurt me?" He tried to laugh, to ease the tension of the moment, but the sound was flat and unconvincing.

"I wish things were different," she said. "I wish—"

"You don't have to explain, Kate." He took her hand away from his cheek. "I understand."

"I don't think you do."

"I know you have a life waiting for you. I know you didn't expect any of this to happen."

"You're right." She looked around her at the skating pond. "I didn't expect any of this. I didn't expect to ever return to Timber Falls, or to meet you and Maggie. I didn't expect to feel so welcomed by the church and community, or to make friends so quickly with so many people." She shook her head. "You and Maggie have made me feel like I belong. You've given me the belief that I can raise the boys on my own and that I am stronger than I thought." She lifted his gloved hand and held it tight between both of hers. "More importantly, you've reconnected me to my faith and you've shown me the importance of a church family. I will never be the same, Jacob, and I have you to thank for that."

Her words, though they were ones he longed to hear from all his parishioners, did not soothe his aching heart. Maybe, in time, he'd appreciate what she said, but for now, it only reminded him how much he wanted her to stay.

She was so close—so beautiful—it hurt to know she could never be his.

He pulled her into his arms and held her close, knowing that this was all she could offer him.

It would have to be enough.

Chapter Fourteen

Kate had done everything she could, and now it was her turn to sit in the back of the sanctuary, with the lights dimmed, to watch the children perform the Christmas program, just as she'd directed them.

The pews were filled to capacity and there wasn't a grumpy face to be found. On stage, almost a hundred children stood in their places, the final scene unfolding with the angels singing praise to God for sending Immanuel, God with Us. Mary, Joseph, the Shepherd and the Wise Men stood around the manger scene with the farm animals, while Maggie stood in front of the choir of angels, leading "Hark! The Herald Angels Sing."

When the song ended, the children filed down the aisles silently and pulled battery-operated candles out of their pockets. Flipping them on, the dim room filled with the glow of a hundred lights. Just behind that glow were the innocent and joyful faces of each child.

Kate walked to the stage, where Maggie had remained, and she put her hand on Maggie's shoulder.

"We invite all of you to sing 'Silent Night' with us in closing," Kate said. "You'll find the lyrics on the back of your programs."

Kate began the song and others soon joined in.

"Silent night! Holy night! All is calm, all is bright."

From every corner of the room, and up into the rafters, the song filled the space, lifting heavenward.

Jacob sat in the front pew, his eyes on Kate and Maggie, an expression of joy mixed with sadness on his handsome face.

Kate couldn't look at him for long, afraid she might cry if she did.

His words had played over and over in her heart and mind since the night before. When he had dropped her off at home, she had longed to call him back, wishing things were different. Instead, she had watched him walk away.

She loved Jacob Dawson with all her heart, but she could never stay, no matter how much she longed to be with him. Nothing had changed about her past and who she was. Yes, she knew she was forgiven, and she was no longer plagued with the guilt of giving her baby away—but there were still consequences from her actions. She had known on the pond that if she would have given even a little hint of her true feelings, Jacob would have asked her to marry him. But how could she face his congregation, week after week, or minister to their needs, without being a hypocrite? How could she be a mentor and role model when she had been such a poor teenager? What if the others learned about her past mistakes? How would they ever trust Jacob's better judgment if they knew he married her with the full knowledge of what she had done?

No. It was better for Jacob if she left Timber Falls and didn't allow him to make that mistake.

The congregation came to the third verse and it captured Kate's heart.

Silent night! Holy night!
Son of God, love's pure light.
Radiant beams from Thy Holy Face.
With the dawn of redeeming grace,
Jesus, Lord, at Thy Birth!
Jesus, Lord, at Thy Birth!

His redeeming grace.

As the music ended, a holy silence filled the sanctuary and Kate breathed a prayer of thanksgiving that God had returned her to Timber Falls to reconnect with Him. Maybe that's what it had all been about. Redemption and finding forgiveness.

"Merry Christmas," Kate said to the audience, her voice thick with emotion. "May God bless all of you as you celebrate the birth of our Savior."

The audience clapped and the children began to disperse among the crowd to their families.

Jacob stood and joined Kate and Maggie on the stage.

"Just a moment," Jacob said to the room.

It took a few seconds, but everyone quieted to listen to the pastor.

"I'd like to thank Miss LeClair for all the work she's done this past month to bring us this program."

The audience clapped and Kate smiled. How many times, in how many places, had she received a round of applause? Yet, this time it felt different. She had not performed, but had helped others to shine tonight, and had filled parents and grandparents with joy as they watched their children on stage.

Jacob also clapped for Kate, admiration glowing from his face.

"There are cookies and punch in the Fellowship Hall in the basement," Jacob continued. "Please stay and enjoy some refreshments before going home."

Someone flipped on the lights in the sanctuary and the room filled with the excited chatter of happy children and proud parents.

Jacob reached down to lift Maggie into his arms—robe, halo and all—and held her close. "You did a wonderful job, Mags."

"Did you hear me sing, Daddy?" she asked.

"I heard you better than anyone else." He kissed her cheek and then looked at Kate. "Thank you. It was the best Christmas program we've ever had."

"Don't tell Mrs. Meacham that." Kate smiled, forcing her heart to stay light tonight.

"Kate." He spoke so quietly, it was almost impossible to hear him over the din of conversation all around. "About last night, I haven't had a chance to talk to you—"

"It's okay." She didn't want him to apologize for speaking from his heart. It had nearly destroyed her to know she'd embarrassed him by her rejection. "Let's go enjoy some Christmas cookies and punch instead."

"Pastor Jacob!" Evelyn Ramsey stepped out of the crowd, wearing a bright red dress with Christmas tree earrings that lit up and blinked. "I've saved a spot for you at one of the tables set up in the Fellowship Hall downstairs."

Immediately, Kate's skin prickled at the sight and sound of the other woman, but she knew she needed to let Jacob go. "Go ahead," she said to him. "I have some things I need to wrap up in here and then I plan to get the boys to take them downstairs for cookies."

"I'll help you get them," he offered.

She shook her head and didn't meet his gaze. "I'll ask a couple of the teenagers to help. You have to get to the Fellowship Hall to visit with all the guests." She put her hand on Maggie's back and smiled at the little girl. "Go and have some fun with your friends."

With that, Kate walked across the stage, pretending not to hear the parents as they called out for her to stop so they could thank her for working with their children.

More than anything, she wanted to leave the sanctuary and be with the boys. She didn't want to face anyone, because she didn't think she could hold up the pretense that she was happy any longer. The thought of joining two or three hundred people in the basement made her feel overwhelmed. Even if they didn't know it, she would know that she was saying goodbye, and it would only make things more difficult.

Instead of joining the others in the basement, Kate started toward the nursery.

"Kate." A woman's voice stopped Kate in the hall. When she turned to see who had called her name, she saw the unmistakable blinking earrings.

Evelyn walked toward her with confident, sure steps.

"I don't mean to bother you," Evelyn said. "But I wanted to let you know that I was very impressed with the program tonight."

Kate tried not to look impatient. "Thank you."

"And I wanted to get some pointers." She dipped her head, false humility tinting her voice. "Since Jacob asked me to take it over from now on."

It shouldn't matter, Kate told herself—but it did.

"You know," Evelyn continued, "I think it's a good idea you're leaving—for Jacob's sake—and for the sake of the church."

"How do you know I'm leaving?"

"It's obvious. I can see it in your face, and I've heard from more than one person that they've seen dozens of boxes leaving your house." She shrugged, as if none of it mattered to her. "But why wouldn't you leave? You're an actress. You have a life outside of Timber Falls." She laughed and shook her head. "All of us knew from the beginning that you didn't fit in here. It was just a matter of time before you left."

Kate tried to force her face to remain emotionless, but she couldn't stop her lips from trembling.

"I just think it was in poor taste that you tried to manipulate our pastor's heart while you were here." Evelyn shook her head and narrowed her eyes. "Was it part of the act? Play the doting guardian, win over the handsome pastor and receive the accolades from his church?"

"Act?" Kate pulled back. "I never tried to—"

"I saw you preening under their applause tonight. Are you so insecure that you need praise everywhere you go, even when you're not on stage?"

Kate's mouth fell open in astonishment. "I never—"

"It hardly matters anymore. Your performance has ended." Evelyn lifted her shoulders and pasted a smile on her overly bright red lips. "You're leaving and now I'm here to pick up the pieces of Jacob's broken heart." Her eyes turned cold. "I suppose I'll be the encore performance."

Kate had had enough. "I should leave."

"Yes, you should." It was the first time Evelyn's real intentions showed through her pitiful act.

Turning, Kate walked down the hall toward the nursery, her vision blurring with tears that she refused to shed until she was out of the church. She wanted to run, but she wouldn't give Evelyn the satisfaction in knowing she had hit her mark.

Thanking the ladies in the nursery, Kate wrapped the boys up in their outside gear and then pushed them in the stroller back to the safety of her home.

It was late, and the babies were tired, so she put them to bed and kissed their little cheeks, knowing it was the last night in their home.

Her emotions begged to be released and she finally let them flow freely. She didn't even bother to wipe the tears away as they dripped down her cheeks.

She was pitiful—she knew that—but she couldn't stop Evelyn's hateful words from replaying in her mind. She knew Evelyn had intended to do damage—but there was just enough truth to her words to make them sting. She didn't belong in Timber Falls and she wasn't good for Jacob. She hadn't intended to fall in love with him—and definitely didn't desire the accolades of the church—but it was best that she was leaving.

The lights from the Christmas tree filled the dark room with a soft glow. Kate sat on the wood floor in front of the tree and pulled her knees up to her chest, hugging them close.

She forced herself to push aside Evelyn's words and tried to enjoy this final evening in her home.

How many Christmases had been spent in

this house? How many birthdays, anniversaries and holidays? As she sat alone, she could almost feel the laughter and joy from all her ancestors who had passed before her. She hadn't known any of them, but she was a part of them, just as much as this house was a part of them. They had loved and lost, laughed and cried, rejoiced and mourned. They had lived through several wars, an influenza pandemic and experienced major world events as they played out on their radios or television screens right in this room. A lot of living and dying had taken place in this house, and she was a part of it.

Instead of mourning that she had missed so much of it, she rejoiced that she was woven into the pages of its story—even if she had only played a small role and would be the one to write the end for her family. She prayed fervently that the couple who had purchased the house would love it as much as she did.

"Kate?" Jacob's voice came from behind her.

She closed her eyes and quickly wiped her cheeks. A small part of her had known that he'd come.

He walked into the living room and sat on the floor beside her, his long legs pulled up to his chest, just like hers. He smelled of cologne and sugar cookies—and she worried that if she looked at him, she would turn into a pile of mush. She would not have the strength to say no to him tonight, so she prayed he did not open his heart to her again.

"Mrs. Caruthers and Mrs. Evans took Maggie home and said they'd sit with her until I returned. When you didn't come downstairs a lot of people were worried about you." His voice was low and gentle. "I was worried about you."

She swallowed and tried not to think about Evelyn's hateful words. "I couldn't face everyone. I know it's the coward's way out, but it was so much easier to take the babies home."

"It's okay," he said. "No one was mad—just concerned. I told them you needed to get the boys home and into bed."

"Thank you."

They sat in silence for several moments, looking at the tree.

"Are you ready to leave Timber Falls?" he asked.

No, she wasn't ready, but she had no choice. Evelyn had reminded her of that.

"Everything is packed, stored or donated." She still hadn't looked at him. "The new nanny will meet me at the hotel in Minneapolis tomorrow, just before lunch, so I'll need to leave here right after breakfast."

"Is it wrong that I keep praying for a snowstorm, so you can't leave?"

She closed her eyes, both longing and dreading to hear him tell her to stay again.

"What about the house?" he asked when she didn't respond to his earlier comment. "Have you found a renter?"

She had wanted to wait until just before she left in the morning to give him the note she'd finally written, but she knew that was the coward's way out, too.

Without a word, she stood and went to the built-in shelf, which used to house her family pictures.

Jacob also rose, watching her.

She took the envelope and turned to face Jacob. It was the first time she'd met his gaze since he'd come. The love and compassion on his face were so evident, it took everything within her to keep herself from running into his arms.

"I wanted to wait—but I think you should have this now." She extended the envelope to him.

He took it, a frown marring his forehead, and looked at her with questions in his eyes. "What is it?"

Sitting on the couch, she nodded at him. "Open it."

He sat next to her and lifted the flap to pull out the piece of paper.

"'Jacob,'" he read aloud. "'There are no words to express how much you mean to me or how thankful I am that I've had this chance to meet you.'"

Kate closed her eyes, wishing he would not read it aloud, yet she didn't want to tell him to stop.

"'I don't know why God chose to take Tabby and Adam, or why He chose me to care for the boys—but what I do know is that He is sovereign and good. You've taught me that.'" Jacob paused, his voice tight with emotion. He shook his head. "Kate—"

"Keep reading." She laid her hand on his arm and met his gaze, tears in her eyes. "Please."

He took a deep breath and continued, "'I don't know how I will ever repay you or this community. I've grown to love all of you as if I've known you my whole life.'"

Jacob laid his hand over hers and she stared at it while he read.

"'My family home is the only thing I possess that has any real value—'" Jacob paused again. "Kate, you know that's not true."

"Jacob." She closed her eyes, shaking her head. "Please finish."

"'The house has been a blessing to my family for over a hundred years, but now it's time to say goodbye and pass the blessing on to someone else. I have sold the home to a couple who plan to move it to a piece of property on the river.'" He stopped reading and met her gaze.

She tried not to flinch or show how much it hurt to say goodbye to the house. She wanted him to think she was confident in this decision.

He continued to read. "'I pray they love it as much as I have and use it to bless others. The land that the house currently sits on, as well as the money from the sale, I am donating to the church. Please use the land and the money for your school. This is the only way I can think to repay you for your selfless generosity. Love, Kate.'"

He lowered the letter onto his lap and didn't speak for several heartbeats.

Finally, he turned to her, searching her eyes and looking deep into her heart.

She forced herself not to cry—to look at him, as he looked at her, and to memorize every line of his dear face.

"You don't have to do this," he said quietly.

"I want to."

Reaching up, he gently caressed the side of her face, love and devotion in the recesses of his gaze.

Kate closed her eyes and leaned into his hand, savoring the feeling of his gentle touch.

Without a word, he lowered his lips to hers.

She inhaled the scent of him and did not pull away. His kiss was tender and full of love, and she received it with all her heart, kissing him back in return. It wasn't a passionate kiss, or even a desperate one, but it was full of all they had become to one another. He held her gently in his arms, hugging her to himself, making her feel protected and wanted.

When he finally pulled away, she offered him a gentle smile.

"You don't have to repay me, Kate." He loosened his hold, though he still held her. "I didn't help you so I could get something in return."

"I know." She looked at the letter she had written and nodded. "You did it out of the kindness of your heart—and now I want to do this for the same reason." She looked at him again. "Will you accept this farewell gift?"

"If this is what you want." Slowly, he returned the letter to the envelope and stood. "I'll see you in the morning to say goodbye."

With those final words, Jacob left her house for the last time—and didn't look back.

The sky was gray and overcast the next morning as Jacob and Maggie stood near Kate's minivan in her driveway. A snowstorm was expected to hit in the afternoon, so Kate was especially anxious to get on the road.

Joy and Chase had also come to say good-bye. Joy stood near the back of the minivan with Kate, talking gently and quietly. Aiken, Bryce and Carter were already in their car seats, Carter complaining loudly that he didn't want to be there.

Maggie had said goodbye to each of the boys inside the house, before the adults had brought them out to the car. She had tried, valiantly, not to cry, but Jacob could see how much it had cost his daughter. Her eyes were downcast and her lips were pressed together.

The air had turned bitter cold in front of the storm. Already, Jacob's hands and feet hurt from the exposure. He would need to get Maggie into the warmth of their house soon, though she was all bundled up in her thickest outdoor clothing.

Joy hugged Kate and then stepped away from the minivan to join her husband.

Kate turned to Jacob and Maggie, her eyes shimmering with tears.

The memory of their kiss the night before was branded on Jacob's heart. She had returned his affection, and in that moment, he knew she cared for him more than he'd realized. But she had still decided to leave. Part of him wanted to talk to her again—ask her why she felt she couldn't stay, and then try to convince her she was wrong—but the other part knew he needed to offer her the gift of free will. He had told her he wanted her to stay, had shown her how much he cared for her in his kiss and done everything he could think to make her feel welcome. There was nothing left to do but say goodbye.

Maggie left Jacob's side and ran into Kate's arms. "Goodbye," Maggie said through her tears as she hugged Kate. "I'm going to miss you."

Kate hugged Maggie back, a tear running down her cheek.

Jacob couldn't watch. It was too hard.

"Come, Maggie," Joy said to the little girl. "Let's go back inside and warm up for a bit."

Pulling away, Maggie looked up at Kate. "I love you."

"I love you, too," Kate replied. "Don't forget to sing and dance and be in as many plays as you can. Someday I'll see you on Broadway."

The words brightened Maggie's eyes for a moment, and then she left Kate and joined Joy and Chase, who brought her inside Kate's house.

Turning to Jacob, Kate bit her bottom lip and shook her head. "I told you I hate goodbyes. Could there be anything worse in this world?"

Jacob had faced many heart-wrenching goodbyes in his life, and this one was close to the top of the list. He opened his arms for her and she came to him.

He held her for a long time, neither one speaking, because everything had been said.

"Thank you." She pulled back to look at him. "I—" She paused and shook her head again. "I should go."

"Goodbye, Kate." He placed a kiss on her forehead, lingering for a moment before letting her go. "May God bless and keep you."

She nodded and wiped at her tears, and then she walked away from him and got into the minivan.

Without another word—or a goodbye—Kate left Timber Falls.

Jacob watched until the minivan was out of sight and then he slowly walked into the kitchen, his heart heavier than it had been since the day he'd said goodbye to Laura.

Joy and Chase stood with Maggie in the living room.

Kate had left the Christmas tree and the couch, asking Jacob to find a home for them and a few other pieces of furniture she had used until today. But the rest of the house was empty. It echoed, like it had never echoed before.

"Well." Joy looked around the house, her face and voice just as heavy as Jacob's heart. Her gaze landed on her husband. "I suppose we should get home to the children."

"Thank you for all your help," Jacob told the Ashers. "I'm so grateful for your friendship."

Joy gave him a hug and Chase shook his hand.

"Kind of funny how life works," Joy mused just before leaving. "Six weeks ago, we didn't know Kate—and now I wonder what we'll do without her."

Maggie stood near the entrance to the toy room, her lips turned down.

Jacob put his hand on her shoulder and said, "I think Mags and I need to go get a treat."

She turned her mournful eyes to Jacob and shook her head. "I just want to go home, Daddy."

He nodded and they followed Joy and Chase out of the house. Jacob used the keys Kate had given him and locked the place up, and then they waved goodbye to the Ashers, who pulled away from the curb in their large conversion van.

It was just Jacob and Maggie again as they walked across the street to their house.

Pushing open the door, it creaked in welcome. It was Saturday and Maggie's Christmas break had just begun. Her grandparents wouldn't arrive until Christmas Eve on Tuesday, so there would be a lot of empty time to fill until then.

Neither one spoke as they took off their coats and boots. Maggie didn't run off to play in her room, but stayed right beside Jacob as he walked into the back parlor.

"Would you like to watch a movie?" he asked her.

She shook her head.

"Would you like to play a game?"

"No, thank you."

He sat on his desk chair and she climbed into his lap. "What would you like to do, sweetheart?"

Maggie looked up into Jacob's eyes, tears in her own. "Can we watch Kate on YouTube?"

Jacob closed his eyes briefly. It was the last thing he wanted to do.

"Please, Daddy?" She snuggled in closer to him and he couldn't say no.

He turned on his laptop and pulled up the internet browser. Typing in her name, he clicked Return and several links appeared. At the top was a news release from the producers of the Broadway tour and the headline said, *Kate LeClair returns as Fantine on 23 December in Minneapolis.*

"Daddy?"

"Yes, Mags?"

"Did you buy me tickets to see Kate on stage for Christmas?"

"No, baby, I didn't."

She let out a disappointed sigh. "What if I never get a chance to see her on stage again?"

"I don't even know if there are tickets available. It's not easy to get them at the last minute."

Her eyes brightened. "Can we check?"

What would it hurt to check? He clicked on the link for tickets to the Orpheum Theatre in Minneapolis, and followed all the prompts to land him on Monday evening's performance.

"How many seats are in the theater?" Maggie asked, leaning forward, the first spark of excitement returning to her since yesterday.

"Two thousand six hundred," Jacob read, as he lifted his eyebrows at the number.

"And there aren't any seats left?" Maggie frowned.

"Well, affordable seats."

"Are you checking?"

"Yes." He clicked on Tickets.

After a few seconds, she asked, "Are there seats left?"

There were a few available, mostly in the balcony—but there were also two available near the stage. Jacob clicked on them and frowned at the price. He'd expected an astronomical fee—but they were decently priced. A note on the bottom said they had an impeded view of the stage, which probably explained the reduced price.

"Did you find some?" Maggie wiggled with excitement. "Can we go, Daddy? Please?"

How many chances would they get to see

Kate on stage? Probably not many. What would it hurt to go? Kate would never need to know they were there—and it would be something Maggie would remember for the rest of her life. It wasn't every day that they knew one of the main actresses in a Broadway show.

Without giving it a second thought, he clicked Purchase. Monday night was the night before Christmas Eve—his one day this week that he wasn't needed at church, and the day before his parents and in-laws arrived.

"Daddy?" Maggie pulled on his sleeve. "Are we going?"

He finished the purchase and was sent to the confirmation page.

"Yes." He smiled at Maggie. "We are going."

Maggie leaped off his lap and jumped up and down, cheering. "I need to wear a pretty dress." She raced toward the door.

"It's not for three more days, Mags."

She laughed and ran out of the room.

Jacob leaned back in his chair, pain and disappointment still heavy in his heart. He was happy for Maggie, but he knew how much of a toll it would be on him to watch Kate on stage.

At some point, he would have to say goodbye for good.

Seeing Kate again felt like it was only prolonging his agony.

Chapter Fifteen

Nerves bubbled in Kate's stomach as she stood in the wings of the stage, wearing her costume. The long simple gray gown was covered by a smudged apron and she wore a dirtied mobcap on her head. She watched James playing Jean Valjean as he received the bishop's pardon and then sang "What Have I Done?"

The audience's response to the earlier scenes had been powerful. Kate had heard it in her dressing room as Peg, her makeup artist and friend, finished her hair.

"A good crowd tonight," Peg had said to Kate, looking at her in the mirror. "A lot of people are excited to have you back."

Now, as Kate waited for her cue to enter the stage, she couldn't focus on anything other than the pain gripping her heart. She had left Aiken, Bryce and Carter at the hotel with their new nanny, Mia. She could still hear their cries echoing in her heart as she'd walked out the door. Though Mia had been with them for three days, the boys weren't used to her yet and were still unsure about the hotel suite. They had called for Kate and her heart had torn in two, knowing how much they had gone through in the past two months since losing their real mother. She hated to think they were worried that they'd lose her, too.

James sang with such passion on stage, the song seeped inside Kate and she had to take several deep breaths.

Her mind returned to Jacob, as it had countless times since she'd left Timber Falls. Every memory from her time with him and Maggie had replayed in her heart and mind, swirling together, filling her with the most bittersweet emotions she'd ever experienced.

Before going to Timber Falls, Kate had always believed the only place she could feel like herself was on stage. But now, with the stage right before her, she suddenly felt like an imposter. She only pretended on stage—but in Timber Falls, Jacob had invited her to be herself for the first time—and had accepted her, just as she was.

The stage lights went down as James finished

his solo, and the audience went wild with applause.

James jogged off the stage and winked at Kate. "Your turn, Sunshine."

Kate's castmates smiled excitedly at her as the set was quickly changed for the factory scene where Fantine's character would be introduced.

The stage manager nodded at the women and Kate took a deep breath.

It was time to return to the show.

A cool brush of air blew across Kate's face as she quickly took her place behind the faux-brick pillar that would represent the gate of the factory. Her heart hammered and her breath was short and shallow. In a moment, the lights would come up again, and it would be her turn to perform.

She waited for the flutter of excitement that always came a moment before she began—but this time it didn't come. In its place was a void—deep and cavernous—that shook her to her core.

What had happened to her? Where was the spark of joy that used to fill her when she performed?

The orchestra played the stirring overture, while above her head, on the black screen, the words *1823, Montreuil-sur-Mer* appeared. Stage fog billowed around her, piercing her nose and stinging her eyes with the sickeningly sweet fragrance. The music changed and a dozen castmates started to sing "At the End of the Day." The lights turned on at the back of the stage and shined through the bars of the gate onto those singing the depressing song. Slowly, the light shifted to blue and another dozen cast members joined those on stage.

The set began to turn and Kate bowed her head to pray for peace. She stepped away from the pillar toward the worktable as everyone but the factory workers walked off stage, their song dying on their lips.

Nicholas, who played the foreman, began to sing, addressing a character at the gate before he turned to leer at Kate.

Her instincts immediately took over and she lowered her eyes to assume the character of Fantine, though Evelyn's leer from the night of the Christmas program filled her mind.

The other women on stage began to mock Fantine and Kate forced every thought away but her performance. She pulled the letter from her pocket that would become a key piece of the scene and gave herself fully to her character.

Les Misérables proceeded as it had a thousand times before, in the thirty-four years it had been performed in English.

Soon, it was time for Kate's solo. She wore her long gray gown, the apron and mobcap gone, her hair draping over her shoulders. She sat in the middle of the stage, nothing but darkness all around her as the orchestra began to play "I Dreamed a Dream." The lights rose, and it was just Kate and her voice.

She allowed the music to carry her along, singing from her pain and heartache. Every time she'd ever sung this song on stage, she'd thought of the day she told her high school boyfriend she was pregnant and he had left her alone.

She gripped her gown as the words poured from the deepest places within her. The theater was dark and she could only see the first few rows of seats. As always, her eyes wandered over the faces as she searched for her daughter. It had become so much a part of this song and this moment, she hardly realized she did it until her eyes rested on the sweetest, most familiar face she'd ever seen, and the tears streamed down her cheeks freely.

Maggie.

Kate almost didn't want to find the other face she knew she'd see, but as the words of the song lifted off her lips, she met Jacob's gaze and her heart expanded until she was afraid it would burst from her chest.

Love and sadness radiated from Jacob as he

silently watched her sing. She could not look away from him, her love for him pulling her heart toward him, though the distance between them was great.

Her song ended and the lights went dark. The roar from the audience pounded in Kate's chest as she hung her head, the tears going unchecked. She was afraid her legs would not work, but the show would continue, whether or not her heart was breaking. She stood and left the stage. The hardest part of her character's story yet to come.

With tears on her cheeks, Kate continued to portray Fantine, unable to address all the emotions and feelings swirling through her, knowing that Jacob had come. She refused to let herself stop for even a moment until Fantine breathed her last breath on stage and Jean Valjean promised to rescue her daughter, Cosette, from the Thénardiers.

Leaving the stage, Kate walked slowly toward her dressing room, the emotional onslaught hitting her with its full force. She still had almost two hours before the final scene, where she would appear to walk Jean Valjean home to God.

Her hands shook from the toll it had taken to perform her scenes. She had forced herself not to look at Jacob and Maggie again, but now she wanted nothing more than to see them, to hug Maggie and be held by Jacob.

Before she arrived at the dressing room, she stopped to talk to her producer who sat with her laptop in the green room. After a quick chat, Kate continued to the dressing room. It was almost empty as most of the cast was still on stage, or waiting to be on stage. Kate went to her bag and pulled out her cell phone. So many times these past three days she had checked to see if Jacob had called or texted. But there had been no word from him.

Why hadn't he told her they would be here tonight? Had he not wanted her to know? If not, then why had they sat so close to the stage?

She opened her text app and found his last message. It had been from Saturday morning, before she'd left. He wanted to know what time to come and say goodbye. She'd responded eight thirty.

Touching the text box, the cursor blinked at her and she wondered at the wisdom in sending him a message now. But how could she not? How could they be so close and not speak to one another?

I was surprised and overjoyed to see you in the audience.

She typed the words, wondering if he'd even see them before the show ended.

I've spoken to my producer and she's sending two passes for you and Maggie to come backstage, if you'd like. Just go to the stage door, outside and to the left of the main doors, when you're ready. I'll be here waiting.

She didn't think twice, or even reread the message, before pressing Send.

Since Kate's last scene as Fantine, Jacob sat motionless in the audience. The seats he and Maggie occupied were not perfect, and they couldn't see parts of the stage, but they had seen everything he'd come to see.

They had seen Kate.

Jacob had never watched *Les Misérables* on stage and he was blown away. The music, the actors, the set—all of it was spectacular. But his favorite scene, by far, was Kate alone on the stage. It wasn't necessary to have anything else but her.

In that moment, as her gaze touched his, his chest had filled to overflowing with love and amazement at her talent and confidence. How had he ever thought he could be enough for her?

The room had exploded with applause at the

end of her song and Jacob felt small and insignificant in her enormous world.

Yet—he was in love with her, and even though he didn't feel worthy of her love, he had to tell her. Somewhere, somehow, he would tell her.

Part of him was ready to leave as soon as Kate was finished—but one look at his daughter, and he knew she was there to stay.

Maggie's eyes had lit up at the opening overture and had not dimmed since. When she had seen Kate on stage, she jumped in her seat and he'd had to whisper for her to quiet.

Jacob's phone vibrated with a message. It was in his coat pocket where he'd put it after taking photos of Maggie out near the marquee when they had arrived. He didn't want to be rude and check the message, but one of his parishioners in the hospital had taken a turn for the worse yesterday and he'd asked her daughter to message him if she needed anything.

While the Thénardiers sang "Master of the House," Jacob slipped his phone just over the edge of his pocket to see who had sent the message and his heart started to race at seeing Kate's name.

How many times, since Saturday, had he checked to see if she'd called or texted? At least a dozen.

He read her text now, and then read it again

to make sure he understood what she was telling him. She had invited them to come backstage—and said that she'd be waiting for them.

Had his chance to tell her he loved her come so soon?

"Mags." He leaned close to his daughter, knowing she'd struggle to hear him over the loud song. "Kate asked us if we want to go backstage."

"Yes!" She nodded enthusiastically.

"Do you want to wait until the show is over—or go now?" He hoped she wanted to go now, because Jacob didn't think he could possibly wait until the end.

Maggie paused as she watched the Thénardiers sing, her eyes wide. "Let's go now, Daddy."

He didn't wait, but helped her stand, bending low so he didn't impede other people's view.

It took a few minutes to get past those sitting in their row, but they were eventually in the aisle. Maggie's dress sparkled and shimmered as she walked, and her hair, which he had tried to curl—at her request—bounced. He'd never seen her more excited or in awe before, and he had a feeling that theater would be a part of her life, just like it was Kate's.

"Can we really go backstage?" she asked him.

"Shh." He put his fingers up to his lips. The

theater was huge and it took them a long time to reach the lobby.

"Yes," he finally said when they were out of the auditorium. "If I can find the stage door." He would do anything it took to find that door.

His pulse escalated with each step, drawing them closer and closer to Kate.

The lobby was long and remarkable, with gilded filigrees and beautiful murals. Red thick carpet spoke of the opulence of the establishment—but Jacob hardly noticed any of it.

Stopping at will call, he smiled at the woman working behind the desk. "Can you please tell me where to find the stage door? A friend has invited us backstage."

"Out the front doors and around the corner to the right."

"Thank you." Jacob helped Maggie put on her coat and mittens, making sure not to muss up her curls, and then took her hand, his heart impatient. "Ready?"

She nodded and skipped alongside him as they stepped into the frigid air.

A gust of wind pushed against them and Jacob shivered, even though he wore his long wool coat. They walked past the front of the theater and came to the edge where an empty lot beckoned.

"Where's the stage door?" Maggie asked.

A loading dock and a ramp were illuminated by a buzzing light but in the corner, under the shadows, he saw a sign that said Stage.

Pointing at it, he led Maggie toward the door. It was locked, so he knocked.

"I'm cold, Daddy," Maggie said. "Where is Kate?"

"I don't know." He knocked again, his heart pounding with the beat of his fist.

They waited in the cold, Jacob's fingers and toes going numb, and he wondered if he had somehow misunderstood Kate's invitation.

Chapter Sixteen

The smell of the dressing room mingled with the uncertainty in Kate's heart. Her phone sat on the table, facedown, and she fought the urge to check and see if Jacob had responded. If he had, it would have buzzed—which it hadn't.

Would he come? Would he even see the message before he left Minneapolis?

What had he thought about her performance?

Slowly, she replayed each scene in her mind, trying to see it how he might have seen it—and a startling truth settled over her. She lifted her head to look in the mirror.

The happiest she'd felt on stage—in her entire life—was tonight when she'd seen Jacob and Maggie in the audience. Knowing they were there, watching her, cheering her on, had been the most overwhelming and wonderful thing she'd ever experienced. No audience member, in no theater, big or small, had meant as much to her as those two people, occupying those two small seats, in the large Orpheum Theatre.

She bit her bottom lip and forced herself not to cry again. She'd cried far too much over the past week.

A text made her phone vibrate and Kate's breath caught.

She reached for her phone and turned it around, her heart dropping when she saw it was a message from Mia, the nanny. She'd sent a picture of the boys as they played with some of the toys Kate had brought with them. The hotel suite wasn't small, and they had plenty of room to spread out, but it wasn't home. Carter didn't have his basketball hoop, Bryce didn't have his blocks and Aiken didn't have all the books he loved. Those things had been put in storage before they left Timber Falls and she'd only brought with them a few small toys.

"You okay?" Peg walked into the dressing room. She'd become one of Kate's best friends on tour and Kate considered her the only family she had—until she'd met Jacob and Maggie and become the boys' guardian.

"No." Kate shook her head, staring at the picture of the boys. "I'm not okay."

Peg sat next to Kate. "What's going on?"

Kate turned her phone around for Peg to see.

The hair-and-makeup artist had met the boys, since they stayed at the same hotel, but she hadn't had much time to get to know them.

"They're adorable," Peg said.

"What am I doing?" Kate shook her head. "How do I think I can raise these babies in a hotel room, moving them every few days from state to state? They're going to be miserable."

"You'll make it work." Peg patted her knee. "It'll be okay."

"But what if it's not?"

Peg frowned. "What do you mean?"

"A hotel is no place to raise children. They should be in a home, with consistency and stability. With people who love them and have a vested interest in them. They've lost so much already—why did I think I could tear them away from everyone they know and love?"

"Kate, you're just overwhelmed right now. You're doing what you know how to do. This is your life—their life now. It won't last forever. Soon, you'll be back in New York and you can start that consistency thing there." She tried to smile. "Besides, we love them already, and in time, they'll come to love us, too."

But they already had a family—a church, a neighborhood and a community that knew them and loved them. Yet—it was too late. She'd already closed all the doors to Timber Falls. But what had her options been? She was an actress. She had a job.

Maybe she shouldn't have taken the boys.

Kate set the phone down and groaned. "Tabby should have never entrusted her babies to me. I'm going to mess everything up."

"She knew you would love them," Peg said. "And she was right."

"I do love them," Kate said. "But is it enough?"

"Love covers over a multitude of sins," a voice said from behind Kate.

She met his gaze in her mirror and her heart leaped at the sight of him. "Jacob."

Without another word, Kate left her chair and rushed into his waiting arms.

"Hello," he said against her hair.

Closing her eyes, Kate held him, inhaling his scent, loving the feel of his arms embracing her. She had missed him more than she thought possible. Not only had she missed him and Maggie, she missed Timber Falls and the friends she'd come to care for there.

She pulled back and looked into his beautiful blue eyes, wanting him to know she was sorry for leaving—for turning her back on the possibilities.

He kissed her, with Peg and Maggie looking on, and she did not pull back. She craved his kiss, leaned into it and returned the kiss with her own. Her heart longed for his and she couldn't deny it any longer. He kissed her lips, her cheeks, her nose, her forehead and then her lips again. She allowed him to shower her with his affection, not counting the cost or the consequences.

Finally, too soon, he lifted his lips off hers and gazed into her eyes. "I love you," he whispered. "I've loved you almost from the start. I can't leave here tonight without you knowing it."

Somehow, at some point, Peg must have ushered Maggie out of the dressing room, because they were alone.

"I love you, too," she whispered back, though she could have shouted it from the center of the stage and not cared who heard her.

"Oh, Kate." He pulled her close again and she nuzzled into his broad chest. "What are we going to do?"

She'd just asked Peg that same question, though she wasn't any closer to an answer. She had three little boys to raise—and a contract to fulfill.

"I can't bear the thought of watching you walk away again," he said into her hair. "You took my heart with you on Saturday and I haven't felt it beat this fast or true again until this moment."

She closed her eyes, feeling the beat of it against her ear.

All the reasons she'd left Timber Falls returned and she slowly pulled out of his embrace—though she didn't leave it completely.

"I love you, Kate, and I want to share my life with you." He shook his head. "I know I don't have much to offer. I can't promise you anything glamorous or as exciting as this." He motioned to the dressing room. "But what I can promise is that you'll have my heart, and my home, wherever that may be, for the rest of my life."

Kate never expected someone to offer her such a priceless gift. She looked at the costumes and makeup and chaos of the theater all around her and said, "All of this fades, Jacob." Then she put her hand over his heart and shook her head. "But this—" her lips trembled as she tried to smile "—lasts forever. What you offer is more precious to me than a thousand theaters or a hundred roles."

His eyes turned bright with hope and it squeezed her heart.

"Kate." He started to take her into his arms again, but she took a step back.

"I'm not good enough for you, Jacob." The truth stung worse than ever. "I'm soiled and stained. How could I join you in your life's work, knowing what I've done? I'm not good enough to be a pastor's wife."

"And I'm not good enough to be a pastor."

Pain weighed down his shoulders. "None of us are perfect. When we ask God for forgiveness, He does not hold our sins against us."

"But the church would. How can I be a role model for other women?"

"Because you can lead by example. You can show them that you made a mistake, but that God, through His grace and mercy, has redeemed your life. It's not our mistakes that define us—but how we deal with them that does." His eyes were so kind and so full of compassion, Kate felt herself being drawn to him all over again. "What happened in your past was not God's best for you, but He used it for your good and His glory." He took her hand in his and brought it to his lips. "None of us are good enough—but He is."

"But what about your congregation? What would they think if they knew?"

"They'd see exactly what I see—a beautiful woman with a heart for God and a willingness to live a life pleasing to Him." He pulled her close again. "Kate, every one of us has made mistakes. There's not a person in Timber Falls who doesn't regret something in their past. I am one of those people. If there's fault to be found, it's within me—but I'm learning I can't let the past dictate my future."

Her heart began to soften as she let him draw her into his arms again.

"I'm in love with you, Kate, and I want to spend the rest of my life with you, Maggie and the boys." He kissed her, this time with a passion that took her breath away. "Will you come back to Timber Falls and marry me?"

"But, I've already sold my house."

"I have more than enough house for all of us. It will do my heart good to see it full—like it was meant to be."

In that moment, Kate allowed every care and concern she felt melt away and she reveled in Jacob's love.

She didn't know how it had happened so fast, but she knew her heart was his forever.

"Yes," she whispered. "I will."

The sanctuary of Timber Falls Community Church had never looked more beautiful to Jacob—and he had seen a lot of weddings there. Soft candlelight filled the room from candelabras high on the altar. White roses, with smaller white flowers he didn't recognize, were used in centerpieces and at the ends of the pews, with white ribbons trailing underneath.

Soft music played from a pianist, a violinist and a harpist. Every detail had been attended to with care. Kate, Joy and the church ladies had outdone themselves on such short notice. They'd had just over a week to pull everything together to be ready in time for the New Year's Eve ceremony.

"Nervous?" Reverend Zachary Sanders, one of Jacob's best friends from seminary, had come from southern Minnesota to preside over the wedding. "Kind of interesting to be on the other side, isn't it?"

Jacob and Zach stood at the front of the church with Chase Asher, who was acting as best man. All three men wore black suites with white roses in their lapels.

"I'm calmer than I expected," Jacob said to Zach—and it was true. There wasn't a single nerve in Jacob this evening. When he'd asked Kate to marry him, he'd never been surer of anything in his life—and that confidence had carried him through to this moment.

The room was full with friends and family, many of whom attended the church. They had opted to seat them on both sides of the aisle and not separate the bride's side from the groom's. Jacob's parents had stayed in Timber Falls for the week to help with the plans and they were already seated in the front row. Laura's parents had been invited to stay, but they had chosen to leave town the day after Christmas. Though they supported Jacob's decision to remarry, and had met and liked Kate, they had wanted to go home. He understood their desire to stay away and told them his home was always open to them.

Many of Kate's castmates and crew members from *Les Misérables* had come to support their friend. The musical had finished its run in Minneapolis that afternoon and they had immediately left the Orpheum to make it to the church for the seven o'clock ceremony. They would have to return to Minneapolis late that evening to catch their flight out to Chicago for a New Year's Day performance, but they hadn't wanted to miss her wedding. Though they were sad to learn that she had terminated her contract, they all understood. Her life had taken a drastic turn the day she learned about Tabby and Adam, and none of them blamed her for choosing to raise them in Timber Falls—or marry the man she loved.

The overhead lights were dimmed as the music switched to "Canon in D."

Maggie appeared at the entrance to the sanctuary. She wore a white dress and had a wreath of small white roses on her head. One of the women had curled her hair and her cheeks were glowing. Instead of carrying a bouquet of flowers, she pulled a little red wagon behind her and inside was Aiken, Bryce and Carter. They wore black pants, white shirts and black vests. They giggled and clapped, loving that they were in the wagon and the center of attention.

Seeing Jacob, Maggie grinned and waved.

Jacob waved back, grateful that Maggie approved of Kate. Not only did she approve but she loved Kate with all her heart. It would be good for Maggie to have a mama again, and Jacob couldn't have been more thankful for the woman God had chosen.

Next came Kate's friend Peg, who wore a long simple gown in a soft shade of pink. She carried a bouquet of white roses and smiled at Jacob when she saw him. They had met the night he proposed to Kate and he was thankful she was still in Minnesota to act as Kate's maid of honor.

Finally, Kate appeared at the sanctuary door. She stood alone and had chosen to walk herself down the aisle. Without a father or mother, she had told Jacob she was offering herself to him of her own free will, just as she was.

He couldn't have asked for more.

She was stunning in a white gown that was just as elegant and lovely as her. She wore her soft blond curls half up with a simple veil over her face. In her hands was a bouquet of white roses, much like Peg's, but a little more grand.

When she met Jacob's gaze, she offered him the gorgeous smile he'd come to love, and Jacob's heart started to pound with anticipation. In a very short amount of time, she would become his wife. He had never dreamed it was possible to love another as much as he had loved Laura, but God, in His infinite grace and mercy, had made it possible.

Maggie stopped near Jacob and three of the church ladies came forward to take the boys out of the wagon. Mrs. Caruthers, Mrs. Topper and Mrs. Anderson each took a boy, smiling at Jacob with an I-told-you-so look on their faces. Mrs. Evans waited on the front pew for them with a bag of the boys' toys to keep them occupied for the short service.

Peg and Maggie moved to Jacob's right and waited for Kate to continue down the aisle. Maggie looked from Kate to Jacob, her excitement almost tangible as she jumped and wiggled.

Finally, Kate arrived and Jacob held out his hand for his bride.

She took his hand in hers and then passed her bouquet to Peg.

"You're breathtaking," Jacob whispered to Kate when she met his gaze. Awe and wonder filled his heart and he hoped she knew how blessed he felt to have her stand by his side.

"Dearly beloved, we are gathered here today to witness the joining of two hearts, two lives and two families," Zach said to the congregation. "What God has joined together, let no man separate."

As Zach spoke about the holy sanctity of marriage, Kate entwined her fingers through Jacob's and pressed close to his side. Her touch sent a wave of pleasure through his arm and up into his chest. He could hardly believe that from this day forward, they would live as man and wife and have the joy of each other's touch and companionship whenever they liked. On good days and bad, through joy and pain, they would have each other. It was an astonishing mystery, this joining of two lives—one that would never cease to amaze him.

"Jacob," Zach said, "please repeat after me."

Jacob turned to face Kate and took her other hand in his, smiling at her and trying to memorize her as she looked, in this moment, love and happiness beaming from her beautiful eyes. He already knew the vows by heart, but he waited for Zach's prompt. "I, Jacob, take thee, Kate, to be my wedded wife, to have and to hold, from this day forward, for better, for worse, for richer, for poorer, in sickness and in health, to love and to cherish, till death do us part, according to God's holy ordinance; and thereto I pledge myself to you."

It was Kate's turn. She also waited for Zach's

prompts, gazing into Jacob's eyes as she did, and then spoke her vows. "I, Kate, take thee, Jacob, to be my wedded husband, to have and to hold, from this day forward, for better, for worse, for richer, for poorer, in sickness and in health, to love and to cherish, till death do us part, according to God's holy ordinance; and thereto I pledge myself to you."

"Do you have the rings?" Zach asked Chase.

Chase took them from his pocket and handed them to Zach. They were simple bands of gold, one larger than the other, with their wedding date and their initials inscribed on the inside. Jacob had wanted to buy a diamond engagement ring for Kate, but she had opted for the simple band instead. She had told Jacob she wanted a band that matched his, and nothing more.

They had chosen to speak their own vows during the ring exchange, so Zach handed Kate's band to Jacob and Jacob slipped it onto her ring finger. "Just as this circle is without end," he said to Kate, "my love for you is eternal. Just as it is unbreakable, my commitment to you will never fail. With this ring, I thee wed and with my life, I commit to love and serve you all the days of my life." Jacob lifted Kate's hand and placed a kiss over the ring that now rested on her finger.

Tears glimmered in Kate's eyes as she smiled

through tremulous lips. She received Jacob's ring from Zach and lifted Jacob's hand to slip it on his ring finger. "Jake, I have chosen you alone, from all the world, to be my wedded husband. I give you this ring to be a daily reminder of my love and faithfulness, and as a promise of my commitment to you and our family. With this ring, I thee wed." She brought his hand to her mouth and placed a kiss over the ring she'd given to him.

He hadn't missed her use of his nickname, or the pleasure it had given him.

"By the power vested in me by God and the state of Minnesota, I now pronounce you man and wife." Zach closed his Bible and smiled at the bride and groom. "You may kiss your bride, Jacob."

Jacob lifted Kate's veil and drew her into his arms.

She smiled up at him, love and adoration in her beautiful eyes.

Then he kissed her, with all their friends and family watching, and it was good.

Chapter Seventeen

The street was dark and quiet as Kate and Jacob walked to their family home through the falling snow. A soft glow from the streetlamp on the corner of Broadway and Third Street was the only light to guide them, though they knew where they were going.

All the wedding guests had gone home, cake and punch happily consumed, to celebrate the New Year with their families. The candles had been extinguished and the doors of Timber Falls Community Church had been locked for the final time that year.

And now, it was time for Jacob and Kate Dawson to take their tired children home.

Maggie walked beside Kate, holding her hand, while Kate held Carter and Jacob held Aiken and Bryce. From time to time, Kate glanced at Jacob and he met her smile with one of his own.

They still wore their wedding attire and the snow was slippery and wet beneath Kate's heels, but she didn't mind. Soon, they'd be inside their warm house, snuggled together against the cold.

"Did everything turn out exactly how you had hoped?" Jacob asked her gently.

"Even better." She was married to the man she loved more than any other in the world—her expectations were more than satisfied.

Across the street, the bungalow that had belonged to Tabby and Adam stood dark and empty. In a few weeks, the new owners would have it removed from the lot and the work on the new church addition would begin. Kate was sad to see it go, but like all things, life moved on and changed. Just like Kate, the house would enter a new chapter of its life. What wonderful things were in store for both of them?

Letting go of Maggie's hand, Kate opened the front door and Maggie walked through.

"I'd carry you over the threshold," Jacob whispered to her. "But my arms are full."

Instead of responding, she simply stood on tiptoe and placed a kiss on his cheek. Jacob had not only offered to marry her but he'd taken on the great responsibility of helping her raise the triplets. His arms were full, because he loved her—and that was far better than any traditions that existed.

The boys had fallen asleep in their arms, so they brought them directly upstairs to their new bedroom and laid them in their cribs.

In just a week's time, they'd not only planned their wedding but also brought all the things Kate had placed in storage over to the parsonage. While Kate and the boys had stayed with the Ashers at night, during the day, they had arranged the boys' bedroom and placed other valuable things throughout the house. Though Kate loved it as it was, Jacob had agreed it was time to make the house less formal. Most of the antique furniture had been moved to the extra bedroom off the kitchen, and in its place, they had filled the house with the less formal, more comfortable furniture that had once graced the house across the street.

It felt good to have her family's furniture in her new home. Tonight would be their first night in the parsonage, but all around them, the boys had their familiar things.

It took a few minutes for them to undress the boys and put them in their pajamas. While they did, Maggie was in her own room, getting into her pajamas, as well.

Jacob and Kate kissed the boys, prayed over them and then went to Maggie's room, hand in hand.

Maggie was in her bed, her stuffed bunny at her side, with a tired grin on her face.

"Are we married now?" Maggie asked them.

"Yes." Jacob sat on the bed and patted the spot next to him for Kate to sit down. "We're married now."

Maggie wiggled under her covers with excitement.

"Shall we pray?" Jacob asked.

Looking around her daddy, Maggie said to Kate, "Aren't you going to pray for me, too?"

"Would you like me to?" Kate asked.

"You're my mama." Her simple response filled Kate's heart to overflowing.

Jacob smiled at Kate and they both took one of Maggie's hands while Jacob prayed over their daughter.

After he was done, Kate kissed Maggie's head. "Good night, sweetie."

"Good night, Mama."

Jacob kissed her, too, and then he switched off the light and closed the door behind them.

Standing in the dark hallway, Kate waited until Jacob turned to face her.

"Does it bother you that she calls me mama?" she asked him quietly.

"No." He gently drew her into his arms. "Today, I offered you my heart, my home and my life. I also offered you my family—and my daughter. From this day forward, she is just as much yours as she is mine."

"And today I offered you my heart, my life and my family—including the boys." She smiled. "I already gave you my home, so as much as I'd like to, I can't offer that to you again."

He laughed and then placed a sweet kiss on her lips. "I can't wait for the rest of our lives, Kate. You make my heart so happy."

She held him tight, never wanting to forget how wonderful this day had been.

"This is just the beginning, my love," she whispered, as she looked up into his dear face.

Downstairs, the grandfather clock struck midnight.

"Happy New Year," Jacob whispered.

"Happy New Year," she whispered back.

He kissed her again with all the love he possessed.

Two months ago, she'd arrived in Timber Falls as a virtual stranger. She'd had no friends within the community or had any idea what awaited her. Within a very short amount of time, she'd become a wife and a mother, with a wealth of friendships just beginning to bloom. She had a home, a church family and a place she belonged. Her life was far different than what she had planned—but it was even better than what she had hoped.

God had been good to her, and she prayed she would please Him with the life she would lead as Jacob's wife.

She couldn't wait to get started.

* * * * *

If you liked this story from Gabrielle Meyer, check out her previous Love Inspired book:

A Mother's Secret

Available now from Love Inspired!

*Find more great reads at
www.LoveInspired.com.*

Dear Reader,

Twenty-three years ago, I walked into the high school auditorium in my hometown and saw the man who would become my husband on stage in a production of *Joseph and the Amazing Technicolor Dreamcoat*. Theater became a big part of our dating years, so when our oldest child fell in love with being on stage, neither one of us was surprised. She not only has a natural talent and ability to sing and act but she loves watching musical theater, as well. This past year, for Christmas, we brought her and two of her theater friends to see *Les Misérables* on stage at the Orpheum Theatre in Minneapolis. After the performance, we were invited to meet the cast at the stage door. It was fun to see the real people behind the characters and it gave me the idea for Kate's story. I loved plotting the story and having my daughter add some of the theatrical details. I hope you enjoy Kate and Jacob's story as much as we have.

Gabrielle Meyer

Get 4 FREE REWARDS!

We'll send you 2 FREE Books plus 2 FREE Mystery Gifts.

Love Inspired Suspense books showcase how courage and optimism unite in stories of faith and love in the face of danger.

FREE Value Over **$20**

Get 4 FREE REWARDS!

We'll send you 2 FREE Books plus 2 FREE Mystery Gifts.

Harlequin Heartwarming Larger-Print books will connect you to uplifting stories where the bonds of friendship, family and community unite.

FREE
Value Over
$20

YES! Please send me 2 FREE Harlequin Heartwarming Larger-Print novels and my 2 FREE mystery gifts (gifts worth about $10 retail). After receiving them, if I don't wish to receive any more books, I can return the shipping statement marked "cancel." If I don't cancel, I will receive 4 brand-new larger-print novels every month and be billed just $5.74 per book in the U.S. or $6.24 per book in Canada. That's a savings of at least 21% off the cover price. It's quite a bargain! Shipping and handling is just 50¢ per book in the U.S. and $1.25 per book in Canada.* I understand that accepting the 2 free books and gifts places me under no obligation to buy anything. I can always return a shipment and cancel at any time. The free books and gifts are mine to keep no matter what I decide.

161/361 HDN GNPZ

Name (please print)

Address   Apt. #

City   State/Province   Zip/Postal Code

Email: Please check this box ☐ if you would like to receive newsletters and promotional emails from Harlequin Enterprises ULC and its affiliates. You can unsubscribe anytime.

Mail to the **Reader Service:**
IN U.S.A.: P.O. Box 1341, Buffalo, NY 14240-8531
IN CANADA: P.O. Box 603, Fort Erie, Ontario L2A 5X3

Want to try 2 free books from another series! Call 1-800-873-8635 or visit www.ReaderService.com.

THE WESTERN HEARTS COLLECTION!

19 FREE BOOKS in all!

COWBOYS. RANCHERS. RODEO REBELS.
Here are their charming love stories in one prized Collection:
51 emotional and heart-filled romances that capture the majesty and rugged beauty of the American West!

YES! Please send me **The Western Hearts Collection** in Larger Print. This collection begins with 3 FREE books and 2 FREE gifts in the first shipment. Along with my 3 free books, I'll also get the next 4 books from The Western Hearts Collection, in LARGER PRINT, which I may either return and owe nothing, or keep for the low price of $5.45 U.S./$6.23 CDN each plus $2.99 U.S./$7.49 CDN for shipping and handling per shipment*. If I decide to continue, about once a month for 8 months I will get 6 or 7 more books but will only need to pay for 4. That means 2 or 3 books in every shipment will be FREE! If I decide to keep the entire collection, I'll have paid for only 32 books because 19 books are FREE! I understand that accepting the 3 free books and gifts places me under no obligation to buy anything. I can always return a shipment and cancel at any time. My free books and gifts are mine to keep no matter what I decide.

☐ 270 HCN 5354   ☐ 470 HCN 5354

Name (please print)

Address   Apt. #

City   State/Province   Zip/Postal Code

Mail to the **Reader Service:**
IN U.S.A.: P.O. Box 1341, Buffalo, N.Y. 14240-8531
IN CANADA: P.O. Box 603, Fort Erie, Ontario L2A 5X3